I0831220

Broken Hearts Damaged Goods

By

Jack Gunthridge

Broken Hearts Damaged Goods

Jack Gunthridge Publishing

P.O. Box 1439

Bowling Green, OH 43402

ISBN: 978-0-615-50462-9

Library of Congress Control Number: 2011910887

Aug 21, 2010

Classes will be starting Monday. I can't wait. I'm really glad the summer is coming to an end. It's not that I'm really excited for all the homework, or for the warm weather to go away, or for the fact that I will have to be that ugly pale shade of winter again. It's just that I'm getting my first apartment. I moved into it today. I think Megan and I have it all set up. We still have to buy some posters and stuff for the living room to make it feel more like a home. I'm already liking it a lot better than the dorms.

The best part about having my own place is that it should help my relationship with Steve. It's not that we didn't see each other over the summer, but it was harder for us to have some alone time when we had to go visit each other at our parents' houses.

It's hard to sustain a relationship when you go from being able to have sex in the dorms (while not disturbing your roommate) to not being able to have sex for three months. I don't want to make it sound like the sex is important. It's just that we hadn't been a couple that long before the summer break, so the sex was kind of an integral part of our relationship.

Maybe I wouldn't care so much about him coming over tonight, except that... I kind of want to prove that we are still a strong couple. We were only together for two and half months before school let out. There was some getting to know each other stuff that we did, and then there was the sex. Okay, there was more of the really great sex than the "we're developing a deep and meaningful relationship" stuff, but the sex was the best I have ever had. When you have something like that, you don't really want to see it end.

That's what made the summer suck so bad. It was texting, phone calls, and Facebook chats, and the occasional visit. I mean, it was nice and all. It's just that you can't cuddle up to a text, or make out with the phone. And it's not that I just like him for the intimate things. But when you are in a relationship, you do want to actually touch the person. Talking to the person just isn't the same as feeling that person being there.

I know this makes me sound shallow. I don't mean to be. I love Steve. I know I do. When I had other guys hit on me this summer, I told them I had a boyfriend. I didn't even think about hooking up with somebody else. I could only think of Steve.

It's just that I know that sometimes couples breakup during this time of year. They can do the long distance thing over the summer because it keeps them from feeling alone, but when school starts, they find that they have changed. It's hard to have a relationship when neither of the people are the same.

If the sex is still great and we are able to talk after it, I think we will have survived the summer as a couple. If the conversation isn't that good, hopefully the sex is still great.

Do couples have to get over that initial awkwardness again? Will it be like our first time together again? I hope not. I would like for us to still be in sync with each other. That has to count for something in the relationship.

Aug 22, 2010

The sex was amazing. It was quite possibly the best we have ever had. We just kind of flowed together.

The after sex was... I mean, he held me as he was waiting for the next round, but he seemed really disinterested in me. I was talking to him, and he didn't even try to pretend to listen to anything I was saying. And I can't blame it on him being tired. He didn't have that after-sex bliss to him where he was totally relaxed and could have fallen asleep. He was just tolerating my babbling about my thoughts and feelings.

I hate when guys are polite after sex. If they just want to bang you and leave, I wish they would. At least you know where you stand with them.

The bad part is that I can't really get mad at him. I mean, I want to, but then I run the risk of losing him as a boyfriend. It's just better to tolerate him tolerating me. I mean, it's not really that important to have meaningful time after sex as long as the actual sex is good.

If you think about it, we're a lot better than some couples. Some couples have terrible sex where the woman has to fake the orgasm. She doesn't break up with the guy because the emotional stuff is satisfying. It's better for me to have to fake certain societal niceties in order to have the great sex. I mean, what difference is it than faking other forms of politeness like asking somebody how they're doing when you could care less?

At the end of the day, all we really want is to have some sort of human contact and to know that somebody cares about us. If he cares enough to fake politeness, then he must care a lot about me.

I don't know. Maybe my expectations were too high. Maybe it is easier for couples to pick back up on the physical parts of their relationship than on the emotional stuff. People change, but their sex organs remain the same.

It will get better. We're going out tonight with Jack and his girlfriend, Brittany. I will see how we compare to them. They've been a couple for a long time. I know they started seeing each other in high school. They're a nice, solid couple. I'm sure they had to go through what Steve and I are going through. If they made it through this, I'm sure that Steve and I will.

Aug. 23, 2010

Dinner sucked. The food was good. I just received more attention from the waitress than I did from my boyfriend. Steve spent the entire evening talking to Jack and Brittany. I know that he is living with Jack and got to hang out with them all summer, but it still makes me mad. I felt like an outcast. Even Brittany didn't try to have female conversations with me.

Jack was the most civil one. He tried to find out what I did this summer and find out about me, but Steve kept turning it back onto himself and all of the fun stuff that the three of them did this summer.

I do like Jack, as far as best friends of your boyfriend are concerned. A lot of my pervious boyfriends' best friends have merely tolerated me. I could tell that they hated me, but were too polite to say so. Jack has always been nice to me. He's a lot of fun to hang out with, and he's just a really nice person. I think he knew I was having a bad time, but he couldn't get Steve to see it.

I did like watching how Jack interacted with Brittany. He dotes on her. When she talks, he hangs on her every word. Steve hasn't done that with me the entire time that we've dated. Maybe it's unreasonable to expect him to. I mean, Jack and Brittany have been dating since their junior year in high school. That puts them together now for four years, which is a really long time.

My longest relationship was just short of a year. James Michael Finch, the first guy I ever slept with, managed to break up with me the week before our one year anniversary. I knew that the relationship had been bad for awhile. It's just that I didn't want to admit it, especially since he was the first guy I ever slept with.

I remember thinking at the time that I really wanted to celebrate my one year anniversary with this guy, even though I cared very little for him. And even though I didn't love him anymore, I still thought it was terrible of him to break up with me right before our anniversary.

I mean, I admit that the break up was for the best, but at the time, I did a lot of things that were stupid. I ended up spending the night that would have been my anniversary with Mark Washington. It was some of the best drunken sex that I can remember, which sounds a lot worse than it really is. I mean, I've never blacked out from drinking and woken up with a guy that I didn't know. I just meant that of the times when I have used alcohol and men to make myself feel better, Mark was among the best of what I was wanting him to do.

I know it's not right. And I wish I could say that I learned a lot from that break up. Break ups, I mean... It was a cycle of sleeping with Mark to get over James and sleeping with James to try to not admit that our relationship was a failure. In the end, I was sleeping with two guys without the other one knowing about the other.

Prom was hard that year. I ended up going with Mark because James and I were just screwing around. He was kind of seeing somebody else. As soon as we broke up, this girl, Marissa Canfield, pounced on him. She didn't care if she got used as a rebound. She liked him that much. Of course, I always thought that she was a slut. And I don't mean that in a bitchy, jealous way. She was just... She wasn't very pretty. There was something about her overly big eyes and crooked nose. You know how people tell you not to make a funny face because it could stick that way? Well, Marissa looked as if she had been pressing her nose up next to a window and saw something shocking when somebody smacked her on the back and her face got stuck that way. And I can't really blame a girl like that for being a little slutty. She would have to be for any guy to go after her. Again, I don't mean that to sound super bitchy.

Anyway, I went with Mark to the prom, had a quickie with James, before going to the hotel room with Mark. You hear all of this stuff about your senior prom being special and magical. Mine was a kind of cheap orgy that I wouldn't mind to forget. Unfortunately my mom has pictures of the prom party. I know that I shouldn't wish for my parents' house to catch on fire, but there are some things that I wouldn't mind to see destroyed.

Anyway, what I mean to say is that I should have learned from that whole experience and become a better person, but I didn't. All I learned from it was a lifestyle pattern that I've been trying to avoid, but yet, I still keep repeating it. It seems like the harder I try to have a healthy relationship, it deteriorates into sex with a guy that I no longer care for, but don't want to break up with.

That's the problem I'm having with Steve. I know that the relationship is failing, but he won't change to fix it. He's going to come to me some day and say that it would be in both of our best interests to call it quits.

I look at couples like Jack and Brittany and wonder how they do it. How do they keep the actual relationship alive? The only thing I can keep alive with a man is his erection. All of the other useful parts just die away. I mean, I'm writing this as Steve is passed out on my bed. He's dead to the world. And I wouldn't be writing right now, but we have sex, he dismounts, and passes out facing away from me. That's not much of a relationship.

I don't think I'm asking for too much for a guy to hold me close to him like he never wants to let me go. I just want to feel like I'm important to somebody. But I look at Steve laying there with his mouth open, drooling on my clean sheets, and I think, "If I could carry on a conversation with a vibrator, I would replace you in a second."

I shouldn't think that way. It's just that... I'm no longer in love with him, but I don't want to admit it. I've had too many failed relationships. I know that it shouldn't matter to add another dead one to my tally, but the cycle has to end at some point. Friends from high school are starting to get married. If I don't stay with Steve, I'll end up with something worse.

I mean, he's not really that bad. He's responsible, gets decent grades, has a good chance of getting a great job, and... is better than a vibrator. At least I will get some enjoyment out of the relationship. And our kids would be really cute.

If I think about it long enough, I think I could stay with Steve just for the kids. Maybe If I go to bed now, snuggle up to him and think about our kids, I might be able to actually feel what I know I should be feeling for him. He might even put his arm around me. And I might be able to fall asleep with the belief that somebody loves me and wants to be with me... and not just for our kids, which we haven't had yet.

Aug. 25, 2010

After reading my last journal entry, I've decided that some of my and Steve's problem might be me and my attitude. Okay. It was after talking to Megan while having a few drinks, but the fact of the matter is that I am going to be the change that I would like to see in this relationship.

I can't expect a guy to love me, if I am noticing things like him drooling on my clean sheets. I mean, that's a natural thing for a body to do when you're asleep. It's not something you can control. I'm sure that I drool on my sheets.

So starting today, I'm going to start to notice that good things that Steve does. It will make me appreciate him more.

1. He always buys condoms and throws them away after sex. He has never not been prepared for sex. And he buys the nicer kind, so it's not like he is being cheap or anything. I don't knowwhy this is important and what it really shows about him. I mean, I guess it shows that he is responsible and wants to make sure that I don't get any STDs.

I wonder if I should ask him to get tested. Would he find that offensive? I mean, if I am on the pill and we are in a committed relationship, are condoms really necessary? Maybe the condom is coming between us. It could be acting like a little barrier keeping us from getting closer together.

I wish I could find out if couples that have unprotected sex have better relationships.

2. Steve responds to my texts in a timely fashion. He has never not replied to a text, even if it was a stupid, "OK." I mean, that's not ideally what I want to hear from him, but it is at least a response. Even his "idk" is a response. A very useless response that isn't even worth checking my messages for. And it ruins the excitement of wanting to see what he said. It's like waiting for the mail to come because you have a package coming and then getting junk mail.

Okay. This list is not working. I'm just justifying the things that he does. It's not making his annoying habits more endearing. I think that was the point Megan was trying to get me to understand.

This was all totally her idea and didn't come from me reading my journal. I will have to think of something else to make me love him more. I mean... To make me realize all of the things that I love about him and just have forgotten.

I bet I would freak him out if I asked him to go t a couple's counseling. We're too young of a relationship. We've been dating for five months, but three of those months were spent apart.

Maybe I'm just suffering from post-separation anxiety. I'm not anxious over the separation anymore. I'm afraid that we won't be a couple after the separation. I wonder if there are pills or anything you can take for that.

Maybe I'm too neurotic and need to stop thinking about the actual relationship and just enjoy him and everything that we are as a couple.

Aug. 28, 2010

Steve and I went out to the bars last night. He got a little drunk. Okay, he got very drunk. He gyrated on me most of the time at the bar. I guess I should enjoy rubbing my ass against his crotch as he grabs my tits. Somehow giving him an erection while he molests me isn't very enjoyable.

Since he was incapable of driving, I couldn't drink last night after a certain point. He passed out in my bed. Of course, I had to help get him in my bed.

I thought the night was a total waste, but he had a drunk boner.

It was the best sex we've had in a while. He just laid there until I was finished and dismounted from him. And since he was passed out, I didn't have to worry about him talking to me and saying things that I didn't really care about.

This must be what it is like to be a man.

I can't say that I enjoy acting like a man. The being able to orgasm and then quit part is kind of fun, but I didn't really like him not being present, except in dick only. It was a kind of shallow sex, even more so than a random hookup.

And I did want to talk to him, even if I hated him a little bit at that moment. I wanted him to hold me and do everything that I have wanted him to do since we came back to school. I just can't get him to understand this.

I would talk to him about it, but there's no good way to bring that kind of thing up to a guy. If I tried to talk to him about it, it would just cause a fight. Or he would zone out, and I would get pissed off. He would then ask me what's wrong. I would say, "Nothing." He would push me for an answer. Guys can never tell when you want to talk about something until you get so mad about it that you don't really want to talk about. At that point, it should be obvious what is wrong. But they still can't figure it out, so press you for an answer so that they can fix the problem. The only problem is that the problem should have been fixed a long time ago.

I mean, I shouldn't have to have sex with my boyfriend when he is drunk and passed out. And it sure as hell shouldn't be the best sex I've had in a while. And I shouldn't feel guilty for having sex with my boyfriend, except that I know that it amounted to rape.

As much I want to try to justify it all the way a guy would, I feel bad about it. Now I kind of have to stay with him to help to rebuild the trust that I just destroyed. But I don't feel like I can tell him what I've done. I know that I should.

Do guys care if they weren't awake for sex? I know that most are just happy to get some. The only problem is that he didn't really get some this time. With how much he had to drink and with me just using him to get off, I pretty much left him with blue balls.

I don't really think the blue balls were my fault. With as much as he had to drink, part of his body was telling him to pee. There was another part of his body telling him that he was aroused. I just sided with the part of the body that was aroused. So in a way, I was really just listening to and responding to his unspoken cues.

I think it is best to just not mention this to him.

Aug. 29, 2010

So I told Steve that I raped him. We then got into a huge fight that he somehow won. I mean, he wasn't even really upset that I raped him. He was just mad that we had unprotected sex. He said he didn't want to get me pregnant. He said he's not ready to be a father, and that if I do get pregnant, he's not going to take care of the kid.

I told him I was on the pill. Plus I told him that he didn't cum last night. I then started into my defense, which included bringing up all of the problems we have been having since we got back to school.

He denied us having any problems and said that a normal person would actually discuss their problems with their boyfriend and not take advantage of them.

And I couldn't really argue with that. But when I tried to bring up our problems as a couple, he made me sound crazy or like one of those crazy psycho-sluts. I just wanted to talk to him about everything that was wrong with us as a couple, and he blew me off.

We're supposed to go out in a few days. He wants some time to think things over.

We're not on a break or anything. I think he is doing a power move here. He wants to act like he is punishing me and make it seem like he is right in this matter so that we don't have to actually talk about our problems.

If I let him get away with this, we will never discuss what is wrong. The only problem is that I can't break up with him after having just raped him. It looks bad.

I have to let this go until he is ready to talk, which is not going to happen. He's a guy. Plus, even when we were good as a couple, we still didn't discuss feelings. We just had really great sex and enjoyed each other's company, which included a lot of physical intimacy and some getting to know each other.

I think we really need to break up. There's no way to fix this relationship.

I will wait and see what he does.

Sept. 4, 2010

Steve and I had dinner together tonight for the first time since the fight. We had hung out together some during the week and had a few phone calls and texts, but everything between us was formal, even when he ended every conversation saying that he loved me.

The dinner was okay. He did everything to make it seem like we were a couple. He kissed me goodnight. Well, he kissed me on the cheek.

Maybe I seemed a little cool. He was trying to be romantic. I just felt indifferent to him and really wanted to break up with him. I would break up with him, but I don't know if I want to be just friends with him, or just remain friends on Facebook while not actually ever talking to each other. I don't think I want to unfriend him. He wasn't a bad boyfriend. We're just no longer good as a couple.

I'm looking forward to this weekend. I'm going to go home for Labor Day. I'll discuss everything with my sister. Sometimes the best thing to do is to talk it out with somebody that knows you and has your best interests at heart. And she will help me to figure out what I am really feeling and thinking.

Sept. 7, 2010

It felt good to see my family this weekend. And it felt good to be away from Steve and all of our problems. I decided to not break up with him. I think I can save this relationship.

This feels like the right decision, especially after having lunch with him today. I don't know what changed about him, but we seemed more like we did when we first started going out. We talked about what was going on in our lives. And he listened like he actually cared. He looked deep into my eyes and hung on my every word. He told me I was beautiful and held me close to him. There was a softness and a tenderness to his kisses. And I felt like he actually loved me.

And as we walked back to my apartment, we just talked and held hands. When we got back to my place, I apologized for having raped him. He kissed me and told me that it was okay and that I didn't need to apologize. He should have been paying better attention to me and everything that I was feeling.

We then had sex, but it was different from all of the sex we have had before. It was soft, sweet, and tender. He held me after it. We just laid there and talked. We then showered together and got ready for dinner.

He was even sweet in the shower. He was more loving than erotic or passionate. He wasn't seeing what he could do with me. It was about his light touches and caresses and him taking care of me. The best part was that he didn't ask for anything in return.

He actually took me out to eat for dinner. It was that nice little Italian place, Cusina DeBenecia or something. It was almost a candlelit dinner, except that there were no candles. The lights were just a little dim, but in a romantic way. And the waiter suggested wines to go with your pasta dish.

After that, we just hung out at my place. He held me as we watched TV.

He's asleep right now. I'm enjoying watching him sleep. He's so beautiful. I know that he isn't going to like that term, but how else would you describe it? He's so at peace. His dark hair is just slightly messed up. His lips are begging to be kissed.

And he is shirtless, so I get to see his pecks, biceps, and the top of his abs. He really is a gorgeous man.

And I can't say what has changed or how it even happened, but I'm glad that we didn't break up. Of all of the guys that I've dated, this feels right. I feel loved.

Sept. 11, 2010

Guys are assholes! I want to take back everything I said about Steve being handsome, sweet, and romantic. Apparently he was only doing all of this stuff this week because over Labor Day weekend, his best friend, Jack, confided in him that he was going to propose to his longtime girlfriend, Brittany.

Well, it seems that Steve has been sleeping with Brittany. When Jack told him he was going to propose to her, he broke off the affair and was going to act like it never happened.

I don't think Steve expected Brittany to turn Jack down tonight and tell him about the affair.

I was out with Steve at the bars when Jack called him and acted all excited about the proposal and then asked if he could speak to me. He said that Brittany wanted to ask me something. When he handed me the phone, Jack then told me that Steve had been having an affair with Brittany since the summer and that she told him this tonight when he proposed to her. He said if I had any questions that I could meet him at the FishBowl.

I casually hung up the phone and turned to Steve. "So you've been sleeping with Jack's girlfriend?"

You should have seen how he was trying to make excuses for it. He tried to act like the hero by saying that he was the one that broke it off. He "ended it as soon as I heard Jack was going to propose to her." What kind of reasoning is that? Who sleeps with your best friend's girlfriend of four years?

He tried to tell me that he loved me and that he wanted to work things out. He brought up how I raped him, which was worse than what he did. He had only been cheating on me since June.

The sad part is that I don't really care that he cheated on me. I mean, I have been cheated on before. Shit, I've even done two guys at the same time, but that was without giving either of the guys an actual relationship status.

What makes me mad about this is that I spent the summer trying to sustain a relationship when he was banging somebody else? And then I've spent the past few weeks trying to save that relationship. When I feel guilty about taking advantage of him in a drunken state, he tried to act like I was the reason that the relationship wasn't like it once was.

Then I find out that the wonderful past couple of days I have been enjoying with him are due to the fact that he ended the affair with his best friend's girlfriend. It had nothing to do with me and how he felt about me. He was just doing what he had to do to keep getting some, since he had just lost what he had been getting on the side.

When I met Jack at the FishBowl, I found him to be a mess. He was still coherent. He was just really depressed. He was so sad and pathetic that I kind of forgot my anger.

I sat beside him and tried to smile a sympathetic smile, but he just turned away and looked at his drink as he was lost in his thoughts. He then turned to me and asked me if I wanted something to drink.

After I ordered my drink, we just sat there in silence. I didn't know what to say to him. "Are you okay", seemed a little inappropriate and insensitive at a moment like this. I didn't know him that well. I mean, I have had conversations with him before, but it was always at parties or other things where Steve was around. He was always very good to ask me about my major, how my day was, and other stuff like that, but we had never had a really in depth conversation.

The one thing I always admired about Jack whenever I would hang out with him and Steve is how he always seemed to think about other people and be genuinely interested in them and what they had to say. Although he was a little slow on his conversation tonight, that quality was still present in him.

"I hope you don't mind me telling you that Steve was cheating on you. I felt you had the right to know."

I told him that it was fine and that I was glad that he told me.

"Do you know... all of my friends knew about this, but none of them told me? I've been friends with him since first grade. And I've been with her for four years. And it's not like they just cheated on my once. They've been doing this all summer, right under my very nose. Even my other friends knew about it, but none of them would tell me."

He closed his eyes, and I couldn't tell if he wanted to cry or was about to pass out from the alcohol. I put my hand on his shoulder and asked him if he was okay.

"Did you know that he was cheating on you?"

"No. I knew that we were having problems, but I never thought that he would cheat on me."

"I didn't even think that Brittany and I were having problems. I thought everything was perfect between us and that she was the one I wanted to spend the rest of my life with. You would think some of my "friends" would have told me that she was cheating me when I told them I was going shopping for rings."

He then pulled the ring from his coat pocket and presented it to me. It was a gorgeous ring. The diamond wasn't too big. It was just the right size for a young man still in college. You could tell that he had put thought into buying it for her. He must have had the entire night planned out for her just to find out that she had been cheating on him.

I wonder if the beauty of the ring is what finally made her admit to the relationship with Steve. I don't think Steve was going to admit it to him, even though he did break it off as soon as he knew Jack was going to propose to her.

I don't know if I was admiring the ring a little too long, but Jack looked at me and said, "Do you want it? It's paid for. I worked all summer for it."

"No, I..."

"Just put it on."

He then took the ring out of the box and put it on my finger.

"See. Isn't it beautiful? While I was busy working and saving up the money for that, she was busy screwing my best friend. And you should have seen her face when I got down on one knee tonight and popped that ring out. It brought her to tears and made her admit that she didn't deserve that ring."

He looked at the ring on my finger and his face changed. He seemed to be torn between two emotions, but he dismissed one and continued, "You know you've done a good job of picking out an engagement ring when it makes your girlfriend cry tears of regret instead of tears of joy. That ring is so beautiful that it made her feel unworthy of me and everything that that ring stands for."

And at that moment, I just started crying. I couldn't help it. I just felt really bad for him. And I couldn't stop crying, even when he tried to get me to stop. How was I supposed to stop crying when he just kept saying that I needed to stop because the ring was bought to make somebody happy? After he said that, I just started bawling.

I had to get away from him. I stepped outside, but he followed me. "Come on, Liselle, don't cry. I've had enough sadness and heartache for the day. I don't need the only friend I have at the moment to fall apart on me."

And then I kissed him. I just grabbed him by the face and kissed him. I don't know why. He was just so sweet and pathetic. He had been though a lot. He made my situation look not so bad. And he gave me some sort of hope that there could be a halfway decent guy out there for me.

He looked at me and said, "How you been wanting to do that for a long time, or was it just..."

I then had to explain to him that I kind of get over failed relationships by making out with other people and that he was just so beautiful in his heartbreak that I wanted to make out with him, which is a very hard thing to explain to somebody that was your ex-boyfriend's best friend when they just got dumped by the girl that your ex-boyfriend was screwing.

He thought about this and then said, "Well, I was going to use alcohol and try to drink my way out of this alone, but your way seems a lot better."

"Not necessarily. I've been doing this since I was a senior in high school. I don't know which guy I'm trying to get over at this point in my life. As far as I know, I could still be trying to get over my first failed romance, but with so many guys in between, it's hard to tell."

"Do you want to go back inside and get a few drinks?"

And so I joined him for several drinks. We just sat and talked about how stupid this whole love thing is. I was finally able to tell him about everything me and Steve and everything that I had been feeling lately. And I heard about how he met Steve in first grade and how they had always been the best of friends and how they would discuss women. And then he started to talk about Brittany and how they had gotten together.

I didn't have the heart to tell him that he was still madly in love with her. He doesn't care about anything that happened tonight. He would take her back right now. And that kind of makes me sad. He feels things for her that I have never felt for anybody I have ever dated.

That's not saying that I wouldn't want to feel a kind of love like that. I just don't think it is possible. He talks as if being in love is like everything I saw in Disney movies growing up. I have never found love to be that way. It has always been sex with a guy you find attractive until you end up being friends. I just figured that as long as you got along with the guy and enjoyed his company that you were a good couple. When you end up feeling like you are just tolerating the guy, then it is time to end the romance.

We drank and talked until it was time for the bar to close. And for the first time in my life, I didn't want the conversation with a guy to end, so I asked him what he was doing now.

He seemed to think about this. "I don't know. I should go home, but Steve is there. I don't really want to see him now, and I'm a little mad at my other friends for not telling me that they knew I was being cheated on."

So I told him that he could sleep over at my place. Neither one of us was in the mood to be alone. He tried to object on moral grounds, until he realized that spending time with me wouldn't be cheating on Brittany. Saying you won't marry a guy is pretty final. I don't think I should have mentioned that to him, or kissed him again at that moment. But even guys that are still in love with another girl won't refuse a make out session with another girl, as long as the guy is currently single.

I don't know what I was thinking, or even what I was wanting. Part of me thought that it would be getting back at Steve. Part of me feared being alone that night. I just wanted somebody in bed with me. If you have a guy's arm around you as you are asleep, you don't feel so bad about yourself. You at least get the feeling that somebody in this world finds you attractive and wants to be with you.

We started off holding hands and continued our conversation from the bar. When we got back to my place, I led him instantly to the bedroom and started to make out with him. When I started to undo his shirt, he stopped kissing me and said, "I should be going."

I then apologized to him. I started babbling about how I'm sorry if I made him feel uncomfortable. I know that he is going through a hard time right now. And then I said something about how a rebound romance usually makes me feel better. I just thought that maybe if we used each other knowing that we didn't have any deep feelings for each other that we could both get over our exes while kind of getting back at them at the same time.

"Why should we feel like rejects when we know we're worthy of love", he finally said, interrupting my babbling.

I did my best to smile and nod. I was too close to being on the verge of tears to say much more.

He then took my hand and looked me in the eyes. "We can be each other's cocoon."

"What?"

"We can be each other's cocoon. We've both been hurt by love, but if we use each other to get over all of our previous baggage, we can emerge from this as beautiful butterflies capable of truly loving that person that is worthy of us."

I couldn't believe that he was asking me to use him and made it sound kind of fun and romantic.

"So we're just going to use each other?"

"Look, we're both going through a hard time right now. If we don't use each other to get over the heartache, we're just going to end up hurting somebody else or end up hurting ourselves even more. But if we help each other through this, we can get through this without having to make somebody else pay for the crimes that were committed against us today."

He then went on to explain that we would put on the appearance of a couple, but we would be friends helping each other knowing that the relationship wasn't going to go anywhere. We would be satisfying each other's physical and emotional needs, whether it was a make out session or holding each other in bed.

We were going to be each other's cocoon, where we could be ourselves and learn to love again. We were going to take our broken hearts and all of the baggage that we have collected over the years and become whole again.

For once I was going to use a guy, and he was going to use me. And it wasn't going to be cheap and meaningless. We were both going into it knowing what it was. He wasn't going to be another regret.

And I didn't regret last night. There was a part of me that wanted to have sex with him, but it was more out of a feeling of revenge to get back at Steve. Jack apologized saying that he wasn't ready for that yet. He was still too much in love with Brittany. And I was okay with that because he held me in a way that Steve never did and listened to everything that I had to say. I think it was the first time I have ever had a serious conversation with a guy in bed.

I'm not sure now what all we talked about. I know we talked about previous relationships. I told him about some of the guys that I have been with. He never made me feel cheap. He just continued to hold me and listen to me. He was interested in me and everything that I had to say.

And I felt good about myself for the first time since I started dating.

I don't know how long we talked, or when I finally fell asleep. I just know that I fell asleep in his arms... and that I was surprised to wake up this morning finding him looking out the window. He seemed lost in thought.

I got out of bed and put my arms around him and asked if he was okay.

"Yeah, the reality of yesterday just came back to me. And the world doesn't seem to have taken notice. Look at how the sun is shining and the birds are singing. Nature is saying everything is fine and that it's a beautiful day."

I took my arms from around his waist and moved them up to his chest and just held his shoulders and neck closer to my face so that I could whisper in his ear that things will get better.

He acknowledged this even if he didn't really believe it and then said, "God, your ring is cold."

It was then that I noticed that I was still wearing his ring on my finger.

"Do you want it back?"

His torment then returned before he finally said, "No, I don't want a physical reminder. If you give it back to me, I will just carry it in my pocket and obsess over it and everything that was and could have been. Anyway, I like it on you. It seems to compliment you somehow."

It is a beautiful ring. I hate to wear it just because I know that it was never meant for me. And I feel like my wearing it hurts him. He seems to go through different moods. I noticed that today about him. Sometimes he is distant and lost in thought, but he will never tell me what he is thinking about. He just turns it back to me and what I want to do or talk about.

As much as I have enjoyed spending the night and the day with him, there is a part of him that makes me feel really sorry for him. He won't talk about what is bothering him. I'm fine with him not talking about it. I'm just glad that I can be there for him, even it is by just holding him and being there for him when he is ready to talk.

Maybe he will open up more to me tonight when we are in bed.

Emo Love Poem

By

Jack Webber

I was going to kill myself today. I'm not sure what the reason was, or even if I want to tell you anyway. I know that you probably don't care, even if I explained the problem, so I will just tell you how I failed. That should make you happy since you like to believe that I'm a failure.

First I prayed to God to just take me. I thought this was fail proof. Plus it's quick, easy, and painless. You drop dead, and that's that. But even God didn't want me. That's how unlovable I am.

So I got in my car and decided that I was going to run a red light and hit another car on purpose. I was sure that I could do this. I was prepared to do this, except that every time I changed the station I heard "How to Save a Life". I couldn't kill myself to a song that is about suicide. It would make my death too commercialized.

Plus, I started to think that I really did love my car and didn't want anything to happen to it. And I thought that taking out somebody else might make me like a suicide bomber. I didn't want people to think that I was a radical atheist or anything, so I started to find other ways to kill myself.

The problem was that I have a fear of sharp objects, so that took out razor blades, swords, and knives.

I was going to hang myself, but I thought that I would rather have people say that I was hung and not hanged. Plus if I came back as a ghost, I didn't want a ghost noose around my neck for the rest of my life.

I was going to use a gun, but I've never fired a gun. If you don't shoot yourself just right, you can end up being a vegetable. I didn't want to chance that and have people feel sorry for me.

I was going to overdose on something I found in the medicine cabinet, but I have a hard time swallowing pills and didn't think that Pepto Bismal would kill me.

I was going to jump off a bridge, but then I thought that the water was probably polluted. Plus I don't like to be in cold water. And I enjoy hot tubs too much to ever want to drown myself in one.

And as I went through the list of every way to kill myself, I found that they didn't suit me. If I'm going to die, I'm going to make sure that it fits my personality.

I know that you think this is an excuse and that the real reason I didn't kill myself was because I'm a coward and couldn't do it. You might even think I found a reason to live, which I didn't.

I just decided that the best way for me to kill myself was by getting old. I figured it's the greatest act of defiance I could do that would piss you off the most.

A Rose by Any Other Name
By
Jack Webber

Bitch
Slut
Whore
Skank
Tramp
Best Friend Fucker
Slut Ass Bitch Whore
Skank Ass Bitch
Tramp Bitch Whore
Skanky Slut Bitch Ass Whore
Trampy Slut Hoe Bag Skank Bitch Whore
Best Friend Fucking Skanky Ass Hoe Bag Tramp
Whore Slut
Love of my Life

Sept. 12, 2010

Jack spent the night again last night. Actually, he spent all day with me. He's kind of moving in. I discussed it today with Megan. I told her the entire story of how Steve cheated on me with Jack's girlfriend. He can't very well go back to his apartment.

I don't think Megan liked the idea of him moving in, but he's not going to be any trouble. He's just going to be sleeping in my bed. And I'll be taking care of him and everything. He even promised to put the toilet seat down when he uses the bathroom. I mean, it shouldn't be any different than if I had a boyfriend that slept over every night.

She said, "You're asking a guy that you barely know to sleep with you every night, and you're treating him like you just got a puppy."

She thinks this is going to end badly because I have a habit of falling in love with guys that I share my bed with.

"What's he going to do when you two break up?"

For my best friend, she sounded an awful lot like my mother. The only logical thing to say to that is, "He's going to float away and be a beautiful butterfly."

I don't think Megan knew how to take that. I then explained to her that Jack and I are going to be each other's cocoon. We're going to use each other to get over the heartache, and then when we are ready, we'll just float away and be ready to love again.

She thinks I'm crazy. I think this is the best thing to ever happen to me. I can finally break my cycle of dating guys that I shouldn't. I've needed romantic rehab for a long time now. I tried to explain this to Megan, but I think I just came off as a little slutty.

Anyway, I think this whole rehab thing will work. Jack is used to long term relationships. I'm used to more flings with the occasional relationship label attached to it. We are perfect for helping each other. He can let me know what it is like to be in a true relationship, and I can help him with some of the less committed aspects of a relationship. Then when we go our separate ways, we can know what to look for in our next relationship.

He's getting some of his clothes to keep over here. It's kind of a provisional thing until I can prove to Megan that he's not going to be any trouble. And he had to go through a lot of trouble to get his own stuff. He had to call Steve and make sure that he wasn't going to be over at the apartment first. I think Steve actually left just so Jack could come over and get everything.

I'm kind of curious whether he will see stuff belonging to Brittany when he is over there. I know that Steve and Brittany broke it off last weekend, but that was before I broke up with him. Now that he is officially single, I would think that he would call her up.

Not that it matters. Jack and I are going to dinner and a movie tonight as soon as he gets back from getting his stuff from his apartment.

I know that there's going to come a day when Jack and Steve are going to have to face each other. There's probably going to be a fight. Part of me wants Jack to just go over and beat Steve up now. I think he would, but his feeling of loss over Brittany far outweighs his anger at Steve. It's too bad I'm not a guy. My anger is greater than my feeling of loss. I would totally kick my former best friend's ass for sleeping with my girlfriend

I know I shouldn't be angry. Getting cheated on allowed me to just walk away from a failing relationship without having any guilt. For once I can say that I'm not to blame for a relationship ending. Although, if I had been different or acted differently, would he have cheated on me?

I Saw Her Again Last Night

By
Jack Webber

It should have been simple enough. All I was doing was going to my apartment to pick up a few things.

The place was empty when I entered. It was haunted by memories of a happier time when I was still ignorant of the facts, but it was still empty of human life. I can deal with the torture of the memories. In a way, I have been thriving on them. They at least remind me that everything I knew was once real. It's the physical manifestations of ghosts from my past that I fear.

I knew that my time was limited, but I enjoyed being there too much to even begin to think about leaving. I looked at the pictures of us as a couple. They were important enough to her that she framed them and gave them to me as a gift.

The pictures help to prove that I'm not crazy.

I should have left once I knew that I couldn't resist the desire to dwell on the pictures. As much as it hurt, I enjoyed it too much. I wanted the torture to go on, and soon found myself laying on my bed and looking at the last picture of us as a couple.

Her smell still lingered on the pillow, and I didn't want to leave her, even after she had left me.

I don't know how long I stayed there in my own private purgatory. I only know that I saw her apparition staring at me from the hallway. She was speechless, but I could tell that she thought I was some sort of pathetic creature.

I didn't care what she thought. She still looked beautiful to me. I would have given anything to be with her at that moment. I was taken from purgatory with a glimpse of heaven before being thrust into the pits of hell.

As I approached her, she ran away crying.

There was a time I could hold her and tell her that everything was going to be okay, and she would believe me. Now the sight of me caused her a pain that she wouldn't let me take away.

I left her in the kitchen…

And left the picture of us on the pillow.

Leaving me with only my memories.

Sept. 13, 2010

I had a wonderful time with Jack last night. He's just a lot of fun to hang out. He's easy to talk to, and he actually listens to you. He acts more like how I would want my boyfriend to act than any guy I've actually ever dated.

I could tell that something was bothering him. He came back from getting his clothes without bringing any back. I tried to get him to talk about what happened, but he just said that we had better get dinner if we were to catch the movie on time.

We made chit chat over dinner. Then I said, "You know, if I'm going to be your cocoon, you're going to have to open up to me."

"You can be my cocoon later tonight when I won't have to worry about crying in public."

He said it with such grace and dignity that I couldn't tell if he was making a joke or not. There was even a slight smile on his face as he casually returned to his veal parmesan and slurped in a string of spaghetti.

I've noticed this quality about him. He can make some of the darkest things extremely funny. It's like he enjoys suffering just so he can make fun of it. I think that is why he won't let me give him back his ring.

I've tried to give it back to him several times, but he just gives me a line like, "It looks better on you", or, "I would take it back, but it clashes with all of my outfits."

As much as he says that he doesn't want it, I see him looking at it sometimes. He just gets lost in thought. He did that at dinner tonight. I didn't know what to do, so I just put my hand over the ring.

He looked at me and smiled. "You're fine. You don't have to cover it up. I want that ring to be seen. I bought it to be shown off."

"What happened over at your apartment?"

Without missing a beat and without losing his smile, he said, "Brittany kind of walked in on me while I was staring longingly at the last picture of us as a couple and sniffing the pillow that she slept on. She ran into the kitchen crying. I would have tried to comfort her, but the only thing I could think of was, 'What? It's not like I was beating off to a picture of you.' I figured that was somehow inappropriate at that moment and left."

I knew that I shouldn't have laughed, but I couldn't help it. I decided not to try to discuss what was wrong with him again over dinner.

After dinner, we went to the movies. The theater was full of couples and groups of high schoolers. Jack turned to me and said, "Do you want to act like a couple, or would you rather just make fun of the other couples?"

So he put his arm around me while we made fun of the kids in high school and how they didn't really know anything about love or relationships.

It hasn't been that long since I was in high school, but I know that how I love and what I expect from a relationship has changed drastically. I was even surprised to find out that Brittany wasn't Jack's first girlfriend. He had dated a few other girls in high school. Brittany was just his first serious actual relationship.

I asked him what made her different that he knew she wasn't a typical high school romance. He said, "She didn't make me feel like a horny teenage boy. I was more interested in getting to know her and spending quality time with her instead of trying to see how far I could get with her."

As I look over my previous relationships, I don't think I have ever dated a guy that has felt that way about me. I don't know if it was me or the guys that I've dated. I would like to think that it was the guys. Maybe they never grew up past the horny teenage boy syndrome. Maybe I never gave them the chance to love me as anything deeper.

I look at Brittany. I don't see anything special about her. I mean, she's cute and all, but there is nothing that makes her so special that somebody like Jack should just make her the center of his world.

There has to be more to love than everything I have read or seen in the movies. I don't know how some couples last so long and never seem to grow tired of each other.

Jack wonders why Brittany cheated on him and never told him that something was wrong with their relationship. He always thought they were happy together. He said that is what hurts the most right now.

I told him that I tried to save my relationship with Steve, but I just couldn't. Sometimes you just have to take comfort in the fact that it wasn't you. As much as you loved the other person, you can't do everything in a relationship.

I like sleeping with Jack. We just lie in bed and have deep conversations. He holds me and makes me feel like I have worth. I know that we are just each other's cocoon, but I feel safe with him and am glad that I have gotten to know him better.

I don't know if he feels the same way or not. I think he is glad to have me around because he feels so alone right now. He is more willing to listen than to talk, although he did talk more last night. He talked about Brittany and how he felt about seeing her at the apartment.

I asked him what he thought about Steve. He said that he wasn't that angry at him. He just didn't want to see him. He said that he doesn't blame either of them for what happened. He thinks that there must have been something wrong with him to cause his best friend and his girlfriend of four years to cheat on him.

I don't see how there could be anything wrong with him. He's not to blame. I think if he would actually talk to Steve and Brittany, he would see that. I know that he doesn't want to talk to them. But they were such a large part of his life that I think he has to talk to them at some point.

Right now he is feeling like an outcast. His friends haven't really taken a side. They just don't want to deal with all of the drama. Jack seems to want to think his way through all of this. He says he can't do that with his other friends since they knew about the affair and didn't tell him. He doesn't seem to be mad at them. He says that he probably would have done the same thing if he had been in their position. He said that guys have a certain code of conduct that forbids them from revealing such things to their friends.

This is one of the things I like about talking to Jack. He tells me how guys think. He explains their inner workings for me. He's the first guy I have ever found that has done this.

It's funny. He will talk about himself in the third person and actually make fun of himself and everything that he is going through. It's like he is analyzing himself and not really dealing with his feelings.

I asked him about this because I found it curious. He said that guys don't talk about their feelings. He said that if I asked him right now what he was feeling, he wouldn't know what to say. He doesn't know what he is feeling because it's a mixture of different things. Guys can't handle that. They can only deal with simple emotions like happy, sad, depressed, nervous, etc. The emotions have to be clear. Any time the emotions get mixed, the guy can't sort it out and deal with it.

He said that is why guys solve their differences with violence. If you're angry with somebody, you start a fight with them. Once you've gotten in a few good hits on the person and dealt with your anger, you can be totally fine with the guy. He said that is what is probably going to happen with him and Steve. He's just more concerned about the loss of Brittany.

I asked him to make sure to hit him hard for me. He then said, "You see, that's the difference between guys and girls. Guys use violence to solve their problems. Women use violence to get revenge."

I didn't really understand the difference, so he explained, "You want to hurt him because you feel he has it coming, but you will never consider the hurt he's done to you paid off. When Steve and I finally fight, it will be as two men dealing with the unspoken things between us. And regardless of who wins the fight, I will walk away with an apology and a hand shake. We will have to rebuild the friendship, but there will be no grudge or fear of retaliation after that fight."

"So if he beats you up?"

"It doesn't matter. He can break my nose, and I can come back to you, his ex-girlfriend, and have you take care of me. It's not going to matter. Everything between us would be good."

"So what's stopping you from just asking him to fight you now?"

"You just don't call somebody out to fight. We're not in the old west or seventeenth century France. You have to let your anger flare, so you can let it all out during the actual fight. You can't do that if you challenge the person to a duel. It has to be an expected random act of violence that just erupts naturally."

I laugh a lot with Jack, but I don't know why. What he says is very serious in nature, but he is so honest and straight forward with it that it is kind of humorous. I think making me laugh makes him happy.

He doesn't make fun of me or anything that I tell him, though. He just listens to me and asks me questions that make me think about what I'm feeling and why. I don't think he means to do this. I think he is curious why I think and do the things I do.

Teddy Bears and Talking to the Moon

By

Jack Webber

When I was a child, I would have a hard time going to sleep. I slept for a while with a teddy bear. I think it was supposed to give you comfort just holding it and knowing that you weren't alone in the dark.

I don't think I ever felt alone, but then again, I shared a room with my brother. I used to try to talk to him. He then got mad at me because he was trying to sleep, so I ended up talking to the moon. My logic was that the moon wasn't going to have to go to sleep. And because it's not a person, I could talk to it while still having my brother hear everything that I wanted to say, even if he didn't want to listen to me.

Somehow growing up, I outgrew teddy bears and talking to the moon. I, however, have not outgrown holding something close to me at night and talking about my random thoughts that I consider somehow important as I am trying to sleep. It's just that now instead of a teddy bear, I hold a beautiful woman in my arms. And instead of the moon, I talk to this same beautiful woman.

Women are far superior to teddy bears and the moon. Women are warmer on cold winter nights. They are also more receptive to being held. A teddy bear can only receive the love that you give it. Women can give love back to you.

Women are also greater conversationalists than the moon. You can actually talk to a woman and get her to respond to you. I know this fact might surprise some men out there, but it's true. Try talking to that woman that is in your arms at night, and you'll get some of the best conversation you have ever had.

Here's another little known fact. Do you know that we can see the moon because it is reflecting the sun's light? I know this is pretty advanced science for some of you out there, but I think it important enough to point out. If you can find the right woman to hold in bed and talk to while you are trying to fall asleep, you can actually have her reflect part of what you are.

When you consider that a woman in bed with you could just be orbiting you in the dark, I think her being able to reflect a part of you is essential. Nobody enjoys a night sky when all we see is the dark side of the moon. We like the full moons that fully reflect the sun's light.

Now, I know you think all of my glowing insights just now have a point. And you're right about that. Never tell a girl that is in bed with you that you prefer her to that ratty teddy bear you had as a child. And be doubly sure that you never compare her to a giant orb in the sky.

Sept. 15, 2010

I'm starting to get a little horny. It's not that I need a lot of sex, or am even looking for sex right now. I've been enjoying the cuddling with Jack these past few days. I just need a little more physical contact. And I think physical contact was one of the things he promised me when we said that we would be each other's cocoon.

I talked to Megan today about how the best way to approach this was. She thinks I'm falling in love with Jack and want to make a move on him when he is still in love with somebody else. I'm not, and I think that would be extremely insulting to Jack. I care too much about him as a friend to ever treat him like that.

It's just that I've been sleeping with him since last Friday. I can't very well help him get over Brittany by kicking him out of my bed, so that I can pick up a random guy to satisfy certain physical needs I have. It would break his already fragile heart.

Plus it isn't going to help me any if I hook up with some random guy. The whole purpose of me entering this cocoon rehab is to stop a certain life pattern that I have found myself in lately.

So now I have to find some way to get more physical with him. I'm not talking sex. I just want a little kissing. A make out session would be great.

It doesn't have to be romantic or anything. He can just come to bed in his t-shirt and sleeper pants and start making out with me. He will have a little bit of five o'clock shadow, which is kind of sexy, especially when you couple it with the fact that he still smells of after shave.

He can start with some soft, tender kisses. I may not be looking for anything romantic, but you don't want to start a make out session with full on tongue action. Tongue is okay once you have gotten warmed up and actually know the guy and his kissing style a little bit better.

I know that it would be easier to make out with him if there was alcohol involved, but that seems like it would make things more confusing for us. I mean, we are just using each other to get over a break up, even if I do enjoy spending time with him. I think alcohol would make us question why we made out. I don't want to give him the impression that I am looking for a relationship or anything.

I will have to think about how the best way to approach this is. I don't want to come off desperate and lonely. And I don't want to make him think that I am falling for him when I know that he isn't over Brittany. I need him in my life right now, and I think I am good for him in some ways. I just don't want to betray him as a friend.

<u>Heartbreak Hotel</u>
By
Jack Webber

I have heard about love hangovers, but I have never really understood what they were. If they are anything like a regular hangover, then I would assume that they happen when you ingest too much love. You feel fine as you are taking it all in. It's fun and intoxicating. And then you wake up with a splitting headache, wondering what happened the night before.

I've been a love alcoholic now for four years. I thought I was having a good time with the love of my life. I couldn't have been happier. But looking back on it now, the time was a blur. I don't remember a lot of it. I just remember that I was enjoying myself and felt good about life in general.

If I had any problems, I would just go to her. I talked my problems over her like I would with a glass of beer and my best friend. And she made my problems manageable. She made my problems go away.

If I had anything to celebrate, she was right there with me. I thought it was because I was celebrating with her, but I think it had more to do with the fact that I could find an overabundant supply of her always in my hand. She made the good times better. She made me forget what I was celebrating.

If I didn't see her for a day, I started to go through withdrawal. I didn't know what to do with myself. I couldn't make it through the day.

After a four year binge, I am starting to sober up. I actually entered rehab the night of the breakup. It seems that alcohol isn't really the answer for a love hangover. I tried that first. It dulled the senses when I still wanted to know that the last four years were real. Altering the senses to try to cure your altered senses puts you in a state where you don't know what is real anymore. There is also the problem with drunk dialing.

To avoid this pitfall, I checked into a room at the Heartbreak Hotel. Some people might think this is sad and pathetic. The ones that think this are the ones that are still drunk on the elixir of love. They can't see that they are the sad and lonely ones.

Do you know most people in a couple are in a couple because they are afraid of being alone? A relationship is insurance against spending time alone with yourself. As much as you would like to think that you are a marvelous individual, a lot of people find out that they don't enjoy actually spending time with themselves. But if we can get somebody to enter a relationship with us, we think that somebody else must like us other than our family. And let's be honest. We all know that our family loves us because they have to. If we hadn't been born into our families and had just met them in the normal course of life, we wouldn't even be friends with them.

So being in a relationship is a confidence builder that will eventually lead to inflicting a family upon some other person that is born to you. That is more sad and pathetic than me staying here at the Heartbreak Hotel.

My eyes have been opened the past week as I have spent my nights with a girl that I hardly know. Before you judge me in your self-righteousness, way up high in the security of your relationship, please consider that I have experienced love from both sides now. I am a fairer judge of the merits of both.

Although I was with a girl for four years and thought that she was the love of my life, I can't tell you what I loved about her. I don't know what attracted me to her. There were physical things, but I can only seem to think about her personality and all of the things that she did to annoy me.

But now that I have been staying at the Heartbreak Hotel, I can tell you that meeting a girl that has also had her heartbroken is vastly more interesting than any girl I have ever met. And it has nothing to do with her physical beauty. It has to do with the fact that she has a personality that is fully formed and not part of some couple. She has her own thoughts and opinions. We can actually discuss things.

Sure we are both recovering from a broken heart, but we are spending time together because we are complete individuals that enjoy each other's company. We don't need the insurance of a relationship to keep us from feeling alone. And while you might think that we are sad and pathetic, I feel sorry for you. You have never been free enough of a relationship to find the beauty within you and within another human being.

You have sacrificed the freedom of your individuality for the security of a relationship. Ben Franklin was right when he said, "Anyone who trades liberty for security deserves neither liberty nor security."

Sept. 16. 2010

Of all of the guys I have ever known, Jack is the most mysterious. I had planned on seducing him, or at least discussing the fact that I needed a little physical contact.

When I entered the bedroom, he was already in bed. He smiled at me and watched me as I walked over to the bed and got in. He then started to play with my hair as he said, "You're really beautiful, you know that?"

I've had guys tell me this before, but it was a move that they were using on me to try to get something out of me. Jack was sincere. It was like he saw me enter the room and noticed something about me that he hadn't seen before.

I might have been wearing one of my sexier night gowns due to the fact that I was looking for some action last night, but...

I've had guys hit on me because they thought I was hot. They've told me that I'm beautiful, but they always did so as they stared at my chest. I've never had a guy tell me that I'm beautiful while actually meaning something other than my physical appearance and while looking me in the eyes.

Well, he didn't maintain eye contact the entire time. In that extended moment of silence where I couldn't think of anything to say, he spent some of it looking at my lips. And he got close to me like he wanted to kiss me, but then he didn't.

He just smiled, gracefully backed away to a socially acceptable distance for two people that have been sharing a bed while not dating, and said, "I just thought you would like to know that."

And all I could say was, "Thank you."

And then there was another silence as we were there together, not even looking at each other.

Maybe I should have helped him to kiss me. I think that is what he wanted to do. And I know that he is having a hard time being intimate because of Brittany. He thinks of her all of the time. I know that he is thinking about her when he's holding me and caressing me.

Maybe that's why I didn't want to help him kiss me right then. It was the first time that he was actually going to kiss me, the person he's been getting to know the past week.

Maybe my intentions for kissing him were more than just a physical need that I had. But as soon as I knew that he wanted to kiss me, I wanted him to take the lead and kiss me. No matter how badly I wanted him to kiss me at that moment. I wanted it to be special and not just a make out session with another guy.

And in that awkward moment of silence as I was thinking about everything that I was feeling and not able to express, I started to cry. If there was anything that I did not want to do at that moment, it was cry, especially in front of him.

And being the type of guy that he is, he noticed that I was crying and asked me what was wrong. Why couldn't he have been like every other guy I have dated and just pretended to be asleep or ignore me completely when I cried? I cried after I lost my virginity, and James didn't even try to console me. He seriously just rolled over and pretended to be asleep.

But Jack.... Jack was genuinely concerned about why I was crying, which made me cry all the more. I was crying so much that I couldn't tell him that nothing was wrong, which only fueled his concern, which fueled my crying. As he continued to find out what was wrong, I had to eventually roll away from him.

I then felt his slight touch against my black satin night gown. As his gentle touch caressed me in a way to let me know that there was another human being there next to me that would listen to anything I had to say without judging me, he started to apologize for making me cry.

"I'm sorry. I didn't mean to... When I said that you were beautiful, I just meant that... Having spent the past week with you, I've noticed that there's a lot more to you than I ever saw when you were with Steve. I don't think he quite knew what he had in you"

And then I turned around to face him. I had to. If I hadn't, he would have just continued to say things that would make me love him more.

"You're fine. I'm not crying because you said I was beautiful. I mean, I am, but just because I was planning on telling you that I wanted you to make out with me. I felt anything but beautiful, even though you think otherwise."

And that was mostly the truth, at least at that moment when I was so confused on everything that I was feeling, thinking, and wanting. There were probably several conflicting truths with none being more true than the others.

And before I could say anything else, he kissed me.

Having had several first kisses in my lifetime, I have found that you can usually put them into two distinct categories. The first is the slow, natural kiss where both parties are thinking about kissing, so they just ease into it. It never feels forced, or like you are trying to get that first kiss out of the way, so that your next kiss will be more natural.

The second kind of kiss is more passionate. A lot of times it is raw and animalistic. This second type of kiss is often associated with the guys that you have just met at a bar. This type of first kiss would often catch you off guard, but you're usually just drunk enough that you don't really think about what is happening at that moment.

My first kiss with Jack was a combination of these two types of kisses. It seemed natural in that we had just had that moment where I thought he was going to kiss me. And I had even told him that I wanted him to kiss me. But it still caught me off guard, even though I slipped right into.

It was probably the most perfect first kiss I have ever had, and yet I... I think he's still in love with Britney. So I don't know if he was kissing me to try to get over her, or if he was doing it because I mentioned that I had wanted him to. He could also have been doing it because he actually thought I was beautiful and felt like kissing me.

I had thought about asking him why he kissed me, but I enjoyed it too much to want to ruin the moment. Maybe I didn't really care what his motives were. Even if I could get hurt later on, I still wanted this moment to be perfect with him.

Anyway, we spent a good portion of the night making out. We also had a fairly deep conversation while we were doing this, but I don't really remember what it was about. I was just a little bit too relaxed with all of the physical stuff going on to pay attention to what Jack was actually asking me. I know that I answered him truthfully, which I probably shouldn't have done.

I think I wasn't used to a guy being able to kiss me and listen to me at the same time. Of course, I don't usually have a guy that listens to me.

And it was nice to make out with a guy without his hands being all over me. He played with my hair and caressed my arms, back, and side. He never once grabbed my ass or tried to cop a feel. He didn't even dry hump me.

And for all of the great things that I can say about him and how much I enjoyed last night, I don't know where I stand with him. I'm with a guy while not being in a relationship with him as we try to get over our last relationships.

The only thing is that I am over Steve. He was easy to get over. But Jack is... He doesn't ever tell you what he is thinking. He's great at listening, but he doesn't talk about himself and what he is feeling.

Some nights he goes into the living room to work on his writing, or he will just sit there thinking. I know that he is a creative writing major, but you would think an artist would be able to express himself better in person.

I remember falling asleep last night with his arms around me. Okay, we were spooning, but he was holding my hand. Actually his hand kind of spooned my hand with his fingers intertwined in mine. We drifted off in conversation.

Then when I woke up at four in the morning, I noticed that he was gone. I found him in the living room. He was just sitting in the dark. I tried talking to him, but he said that nothing was wrong.

I didn't know what else to do, so I just put my arm around him and put my head on his shoulder. I figured that I would let him know that I was there for him, when he was ready to talk.

I don't remember much else after that. I woke up this morning in my bed. Jack woke me up when he entered with the breakfast that he made me. He seemed in an unusually good mood. He was like a guy that was in love, which made the entire world okay. He even greeted me with a kiss as he put the tray across my legs.

"Are you doing okay", was the first thing that came to my mind. It might have been a little insensitive for a guy that had just made me breakfast, but I was confused by his behavior.

Again he said that everything was fine. And I let it drop because I wanted to believe that if he was torn between two women, I was winning at the moment. The more time I spend with him, I should be able to get him to love only me.

I know I promised him that we would be each other's cocoon where we would heal each other so that we could turn into these beautiful butterflies that will just fly off to find some perfect love. But I've been thinking that I don't want to heal him to have him leave to love somebody else.

I've decided that I'm going to perform an exorcism on him. I'm going to drive that fucking bitch that broke his heart from his mind and heal his heart. Once I drive the darkness out, I will replace it with the light of my love.

A Kiss is Just a Kiss

By

Jack Webber

I got my first girlfriend when I was in kindergarten. It was a magical time where a boy and a girl could play the perfect couple. We were young enough and stupid enough to think that love could just be sustained by enjoying each other's company.

In that idyllic state, I received my first kiss. Like my relationship, it was simple and sweet. We weren't going for complex. We were just playing the common male and female roles that we had seen on TV and in movies.

It seems that such a relationship is not sustainable. Boys and girls can't play the sex roles that they've grown up with. They haven't lived enough to know that humans are more messed up than our parents and Hollywood would allow us to believe.

It is in this awkward stage between grade school and junior high that boys and girls first learn that they are better off without the opposite sex. Bros before hoes. Sisters before misters.

And then comes junior high when the girls start to become more attractive. You don't know why, but you want to try to impress them. You start changing your behavior to get their attention. You could blame it on some sort of weakness on your part, but the fact of the matter is that women spend a large amount of time at this age to make men weak. It is actually rather cruel. Men would complain, but there is a certain bliss in the free fall.

It is during this stage that I received my first true kiss. It was at an eighth grade dance. We were doing a little slow dance. I really liked this girl, and not because she was fun to hang out with or because I thought she was cute. We were no longer playing roles. We were getting to know each other.

More than an exploration into foreign territory, the kiss was an expression of something deeper. Even if the relationship didn't last, the feeling and sensation caused by that first kiss keeps us wanting more and looking for more as we go through life.

As we search for more of what we found in that first kiss, we sometimes feel something for the other person. Other times we are just exploring our options with what is available to us at that moment. Our emotional involvement waxes and wanes as we enjoy the physical. There are just the two camps of kissing. We can do it for the simple pleasure or as an expression of something different.

And that is what I thought until last night when I made out with a girl that I am not dating and have no intention of dating. In fact, we have both agreed that we are just using each other to get over our recent breakups.

I know that this may sound cruel and uncaring, but kissing her last night was almost an epiphany. It wasn't an empty, purely physical experience. And yet, it also wasn't an expression of anything that I might be feeling for her. It was…

It was a healing experience where I was kissing her soul. Of all of the women I have kissed, I have never kissed a woman's soul before. This includes my longest relationships where I thought that this was the person I was going to marry.

I might have to seriously reconsider the wisdom of my mother whenever I would fall down as a child. I outgrew that stage of my life where I could fall down and have somebody kiss it and make it better. But as I am going through this breakup, I might very much need somebody to heal the wounds that I can't see or even express.

Liselle
<u>(You'll Never Know)</u>
By
Jack Webber

Everybody has a personae that they like to project to the world. Sometimes this is intentional due to the fact that a great many of us would think that others would never like us if we tried to be who we really are. And then there are people like Liselle, who are so much more than they seem to be. It's not that they are trying to be somebody else. They are just so easily pigeonholed and classified by people that their true personality never seems to escape that label.

When I first met Liselle, I thought she was like most of Steve's other girlfriends. She was attractive, but she didn't seem to have much else to her. That doesn't mean that I didn't think she wasn't a nice person. Steve and I have never really had the same taste in women, until recently. He has always preferred the eye candy, while I have always gone for substance over style.

That is what has made getting to know Liselle such a surprise. There is a lot more to her than I would have suspected. And it makes me sad to think that men like Steve have dated her for extended periods of time and never realized how truly beautiful she is. Worse still is that, with no man ever telling her this, she has no idea herself.

I tried to tell her myself, but I think it came out wrong. She started crying. And in logic that no man ever really understands, she said that she wasn't crying because I said that she was beautiful; she was crying because I told her she was beautiful when she was planning on making out with me.

You see, logic like this confuses men, who by their very nature look at the world through cause and effect. In man's natural viewpoint, when you tell a girl that she is beautiful and she starts crying, it means that there is a correlation between the two. The cause: You told her that she was beautiful. The effect: She started crying. If you hadn't told her that she was beautiful, she wouldn't have started crying.

And as a man, I can tell you that men never like to make women cry, unless they are purposefully trying to hurt them, but those are usually abusive and controlling men. But generally, when you are trying to do something nice like telling a girl that she's beautiful, you want it to be nice. You want her to accept it in the spirit in which it is given. When she starts to cry, the man thinks that he has done something wrong. He then tries to make the woman stop crying, so he does even nicer things than telling her she's beautiful, which only causes her to cry more. All of this further confuses the boy.

What women do not understand is that men see tears and crying as a bad thing. You cry when you are upset, when somebody close to you dies, or if you are extremely moved by something like a book or a movie. But crying at other times than these is frowned upon by men. There's no reason for it. There has to be a certain, identifiable cause for the crying.

So, although I had wanted her to accept my compliment as something that would bring her joy and know that I found something about her as a person beautiful, her crying and reasoning behind the crying really speaks volumes more to what I ultimately found beautiful about her.

When I found out my best old ex-friend Steve was messing around with my girlfriend, who would have been my fiancé had she said, "Yes" when I proposed to her, instead of, "I'm sorry to hurt you, but I've kind of been seeing your best friend behind your back. And I prefer him to you." Anyway, this found me drunk and lonely, which was kind of how Liselle was, too. For some reason, when a man and a woman are both drunk and lonely, it is usually cause enough for the two of them to fool around.

I am not sure what the woman's reasoning behind going along with this is. The man's reasoning and logic in these cases is usually pretty sound. It very rarely has anything to do with the alcohol or being lonely. It usually has more to do with the cold, hard facts of one being a man while the other is a woman. It seems only natural that when a single man finds a woman, who is also single, that he should in some way see if he can couple off with her. How long the coupling off will last really depends on a number of factors, but the man will worry about that later. At this stage, he is just interested in being with a girl. If it doesn't work out, he can always use the "drunk and lonely" excuse. It's basically the dating world's equivalent of the insanity plea.

So Liselle and I found ourselves drunk, lonely, of sound state of mind, and back at her place. We were curing our current problems with an act of revenge and by helping somebody else out that was in a similar situation. Now, I know this doesn't sound very beautiful. In fact, I would even admit that it sounds a little down and dirty, but I… It's not that I couldn't perform, or didn't find Liselle attractive, I was still in love with somebody else and didn't want to do anything stupid that would screw up my chances of being able to fix a broken relationship.

Liselle understood this and was there for me that first night when my whole world had come crashing down on me. She was a greater friend as somebody I only knew through somebody else than some of my actual friends. She was also a much greater comfort than any bottle of alcohol.

I'm not going to say that I was suicidal that night, or the next couple of days after that, but I found certain bright spots in being with Liselle in the days immediately after the breakup. This is one of the reasons that I told her she was beautiful. But it wasn't just that she was a comfort to me. In a way, she defied my expectations and proved herself to be more beautiful.

Knowing the type of girl Steve usually dates, I would not have been surprised if they would have slept with me to get back at him for cheating on them. It would have been the revenge game. But Liselle…

As I have gotten to know her, I have discovered that she felt something for Steve, which kind of surprises me. Most of the girls that he dates are in the relationship because he is reasonably attractive and fun to be around. She saw things in him that I saw in him as my best friend. That's not saying that I don't find the guy to be total dick at this moment in time. But it is somehow validating for me to know that I wasn't crazy in thinking this son of a bitch was my best friend from the time that I was six. It's always nice to know that the majority of my existence wasn't spent having fun with a girlfriend stealing man-whore that puts getting some ahead of his closest personal relationships.

Even though she cared for him, she doesn't seem to be as hurt as I am by being cheated on and dumped. I admit that my last relationship lasted longer than hers and Steve's, but she seems to be quite alright with not being with him. I tried to understand this because I want to know if I am lingering on the past. There is also a part of me that wanted to know what their relationship was like and why it failed. I wanted to try to understand her thinking and feelings.

I didn't expect it to turn into one of the deepest conversations I have ever had with a woman. She told me about the problems that she had been having with Steve since school started and how she had tried to save the relationship. She told me about how she had raped him one night when he was really drunk and had wished that she could have had a relationship with him like I had with Brittany. And then she went into her past boyfriends and other sexual exploits.

I know that this may not sound exactly beautiful, but you didn't hear her talk about it. She never tried to justify any of her previous behavior, or say that she has changed. I think she regrets some of her exes, but she doesn't offer any apologies. She seems to have been looking for love and willing to give more of herself than she should have. It was like she was playing the lottery with these men. She was willing to unapologetically go all in for a chance of something that could have paid off. If it didn't work, at least she gave it her best shot.

As somebody who maybe guards his heart a little bit too much, I have to admire somebody who has the courage and nerve to love as if there is no tomorrow. She knows that by exposing everything that she has to the person she cares for that she opening herself up to heartache, but she is willing to take that chance. I think there is something beautiful about that.

And when I think about it, it is even more beautiful because she has never closed up her heart after having been hurt. She doesn't judge all men based on what one has done. She still thinks that there could be a perfect guy for her out there that will give her everything she has been looking for.

And I don't know why, but with her crying and everything that she was saying, I couldn't help but to kiss her soul. I wanted to make her understand that she was beautiful and that I truly thought she was beautiful.

I don't know when I will be cured from my broken heart. Hopefully I will be able to love again and be able to love the way that Liselle does. Until that time, I expect to have her reveal more of her true beauty and to help me to be whole again. And maybe by the time she helps me to accomplish this; I can actually make her understand just how beautiful she is. Otherwise, she'll never know.

Sept. 18, 2010

Jack and I went to a party tonight. I don't think he really wanted to go, but I thought that it would be good for him. We have basically been isolated from a mutual group of friends. As much as I like spending time with him, I think he needs to go out and see some of his guy friends.

Although I knew that Steve and Brittany would be at this party, I still thought that we should go. His friends wanted him to go. I think that was partly to know that he was okay. There were also rumors that Jack and I had been sleeping together ever since the breakup. I think they were curious whether this was out of revenge, or if we were just screwing each other because of the fun of it.

Since the breakup, Steve and Brittany have officially become a couple. They were Facebook official and everything. It didn't even take them 24 hours to go from being in a relationship with us to being single to being in a relationship with another person. I think they thought it made it look better if they were a couple versus just being two people who were cheating on their exes with each other.

Our friends had already accepted Steve and Brittany as an actual couple, even though they knew the circumstances behind their getting together. Jack and I, on the other hand, were a curiosity. Maybe we didn't want to be legitimate. There is a certain amount of wanting to enjoy that feeling of being newly single where you can do whatever you want with whomever you want whenever and however you want. Jack and I sort of went to the party with this attitude.

We also went with the understanding that we would flaunt ourselves at this party. We wanted to show that we were doing okay. I knew that this was going to be easier for me since I was already over Steve. I wasn't too thrilled about seeing him with Brittany, but I was over him. Jack would have to be the one who did the majority of the real acting. I went to the party knowing that I would have to be his support system. This may not be the best way to go to a party, but it is what he needed.

The party started okay. We made our scandalous entrance. Jack kept his arm around my waist. We made all sort of private comments to each other. Once we proved our legitimate couplehood, we casually went our separate ways. I ended up talking to Megan, while Jack was talking to Dave and Chris.

Megan gave me crap the moment that I was alone with her. She applauded me on my performance with Jack. She wondered whether we could keep it up when Steve and Brittany showed up.

I tried to act like I didn't know what she was talking about, so she became more direct and asked me how I was going to handle seeing the guy I loved show his feelings for a woman other than me.

Megan is my best friend. I love her dearly, but I don't know why she thinks I am falling for Jack and that he doesn't care for me at all, or will ever like me. I mean, I don't love him. I just think he is a really sweet guy. He's funny and fun to hang out with. He's just....

Okay. While I was talking to Megan, I think he could tell that I was getting a little bit upset with her. Maybe it was because I was looking at him while I was talking to her, which he caught me looking at him and smiled at me. But when I started to lose the argument that I was falling for him when I shouldn't be, he came over to me and put his arms around my waist and started to kiss me. He just interrupted me midsentence, and I went along with him.

The best part was that when he was finished, he acted like he hadn't noticed Megan standing there. "Oh, I'm sorry. Were you girls talking about something important?"

Megan seemed a little taken off guard. "No, we were just discussing you..."

Jack then shot a look at me that was a little flirty and playful. "Oh, so I'm the subject of girl talk. Somebody must be falling for me."

I was too busy blushing to really appreciate the look on Megan's face. Of course, it was nothing compared to the look on her face when Jack turned to her and said, "But it's okay. I've fallen for her, too. Just don't tell her. I think she should hear it from me first."

He then winked at me and started to walk away. I started to say something to Megan, when Jack turned back around and with all seriousness said, "And, Liselle, in case I forget to tell you later, you look amazing tonight."

The man makes my vagina hurt. He also made Megan stop from giving me a lecture about falling in love with a guy that isn't capable of loving me. I mean, the man is probably not capable of loving me right now, but he holds the potential. I'm okay with that right now. I would rather fake having a boyfriend with a guy that is sweet, sincere, genuine, and who has actually thought more about me than the majority of the guys I've actually dated than to be actually dating somebody that pretends to love me when their actions don't match their words.

I'm not saying Jack is my boyfriend, or that I am considering him my boyfriend. I'm just saying that it is nice to be with a guy that can sense when I want him near and knows what to say and do at these moments. What I'm saying is that I really like him and that I'm willing to do without an official name on our relationship.

Anyway, about twenty minutes later, Steve and Brittany showed up. They tried to act like everybody was glad to see them and that nothing was wrong, but the fact of the matter was that everybody was trying to find me and Jack. We were kind of spread across the room since I was still talking to Megan and he was hanging out with Dave and Chris. That didn't make it look like we were much of a couple.

Megan warned me not to do anything stupid, which meant that I made my way over to Jack and sat on his lap. You should have seen the look on Brittany's face. She gave me the evilest look I have ever gotten from another woman, which is saying a lot.

I probably shouldn't have been so loving on Jack at that moment, especially since I couldn't exactly read what he was feeling. I think his heart was re-breaking. Any healing that had occurred was now gone. Here he was with a girl that was throwing herself at him while he was watching his ex with his former best friend. He knew that they were a real couple and that we were just a cheap imitation. Well, I was just cheap. I should never have...

I should have been there for him, instead of trying to prove to somebody else that we were a couple. It's just that Steve and Brittany looked so happy. And Brittany looked absolutely stunning. They looked like more of a couple together than Jack and Brittany or Steve and I ever did.

They had planned their appearance at this party a lot more than Jack and I had. We just looked stupid. I probably looked more stupid than he did. After it clicked that he wasn't responding to me nibbling on his ear, I apologized for making him come to the party.

He then looked at me and was quiet for a few seconds. He was searching my eyes, and then he started to kiss me. He wasn't making out with me. I mean, it was a make out session, but it wasn't just about the physical pleasure. He was kissing something more to me than just me.

I was kind of taken aback by this, but I was enjoying it a little bit too much to really question it. It probably lasted a minute or so. I just know that when he stopped, I was left there, on his lap, with my eyes closed, and totally speechless.

When I finally opened my eyes, which was a noticeably delayed reaction, I saw Jack smiling at me. He was just enjoying the look on my face. Dave and Chris were just staring at me and Jack in disbelief. Jack finally broke the silence by saying, "Don't look now, but I think we've pissed off Steve and Brittany."

"So how long are we going to be avoiding them?"

"Are we avoiding them? That's a little rude, don't you think? We should go over there and show them that we are mature adults."

So Jack and I got up and walked over to Steve and Brittany. I was a bit giddy and enjoyed holding hands with him on the way over there. And he was a gentleman- happy, but not really showing what he was feeling. I think he was feeling more for me than for Brittany, which is all I really cared about at this time. That's enough for me.

I've been drunk at parties before, but I have never been love drunk before. I couldn't imagine being any happier than I was at that moment. In many ways, it was like the first time that I had ever fallen in love, but it was more intense. I was more alive, and it seemed more real.

And somehow in the following blur of events, Jack and I ended up competing against Steve and Brittany in a game of beer pong. I think Jack and I were winning. I wasn't really paying attention to the game. I was kind of enjoying the fact that Jack was so amazing and that it was pissing Brittany off so much.

And that is when I received a sobering bitch slap. Brittany noticed that I was wearing Jack's ring. Well, it was Brittany's ring, but Jack gave it to me. Anyway, she still felt that she had some sort claim to the ring, even though she turned him down.

The game just sort of stopped as Jack and Brittany went back and forth over the true ownership of the ring. Jack was firm but civil in his responses to her. But Brittany had it in for me. The last thing I remember her saying was something like, "My God, Jack. You don't just give a diamond ring to the first slut that will fuck you." I don't know what his response to that was. I sort of ran off to the bathroom and started to cry.

Whatever his response was, he must have finished the argument with it because he was knocking on the bathroom door to see if I was alright. I wanted to be alone, but I couldn't exactly leave him out there either. So I opened the door and without talking to him, I sat on the side of the bath tub.

Jack, seeing that I wasn't going to talk to him about what was wrong, closed the bathroom door and locked it. He then sat next to me on the tub and put his arm around me.

You can tell a lot about a guy by what he does when you're crying. Some don't know what to say, so they just sit there in silence and hope that they are able to be comforting enough when you are willing to start talking about it. Others ask you if you want to talk about it and then say that they are there for you when you do want to talk about it. And then there's Jack.

Jack is the type of guy who sits there quietly for a minute, holds you while you cry, and doesn't ask if you want to talk about it. Instead he breaks the awkward silence with, "Do you know the other night when I said you were beautiful? You become more beautiful the more time I spend with you."

And as I started to cry even more at words that I didn't exactly want to hear at that moment, he continued, "The night I gave you that ring, I was lost, hurt, and lonely. My world had come to an end. You were there for me, opened your home up to me, and kept me from doing things I would later regret. And it may not seem like much to you, but your simple acts of kindness probably saved my life that night and for the next few days after."

Hearing him admit that he was suicidal made my being called a slut seem not so important, so I looked at him as he went on, "You may not believe it, but I think I gave that ring to the right girl."

He then kissed me on the forehead and held me just a little tighter. And I wanted to say something, but I didn't quite know what to say. We ended up looking in each other's eyes. And there was that moment where you think you're going to kiss each other. It would have been a kiss that would have meant something.

But before we could maneuver into the kiss, there was a knock at the door. Some drunk guy had to pee. He just kept knocking and yelling, "Come on. Hurry up in there. I've got to piss like a mother fucker."

I looked at Jack and was horrified. I couldn't go out there and have everybody know that I was crying, but I didn't know how to tell Jack that. Anyway, there was no way to stop him. Before I could say anything, Jack was up next to the door and pounding against it as if he was having sex. "Just a minute, Dude. I've got a girl in here, and I can't stop now."

Before I could bust out laughing, Jack motioned for me to be quiet. He then just continued to bang up next to the door and fake an orgasm. But the drunk guy wouldn't be deterred. "Couldn't you just take her to one of the bedrooms?"

"Good God, Man! Do you want get blue balls? Piss outside if you have to. Oh, fuck, yes, there. Shiiiiit. Fuck."

Jack then looked at me and motioned if I was ready to go. I whispered that I couldn't go out there when it looked like I had been crying.

So Jack continued to fake an orgasm as he moved away from the door. "Oh, you dirty bitch. Yes", and then he turned on the water on the bathtub. And when the water was warm enough, he turned on the shower and motioned for me to get in. I looked at him like he was crazy.

"Get in. Nobody will know that you were crying. They will just think we had sex in the shower" was his response to me. And it was so crazy, that I wanted to go along with it. So I stepped inside the shower with one of my favorite outfits on.

Jack then got in with me and greeted me with, "You know you could show some signs of pleasure yourself. Right now it's not looking very good for me."

So there we were in the shower with our clothes on faking orgasms. It was quite possibly the most fun I have ever had. It was just crazy and funny. And Jack was wonderful. When he faked his climax, he fell into me as if he were exhausted. He then fake apologized, "I'm sorry if I came before you did. I hope you still enjoyed it."

"It was the best I've never had", I said finally laughing.

And thinking that we were now good to go outside and rejoin the party, I started to turn the water off. Jack then stopped me. "Before we get out of the shower, I have a sort of odd request."

"You're going to ask me to do something while we're in the shower with our clothes on", was all I could think of to say.

"I know. I'm insane, but I've always wanted to kiss a girl in the rain. It's on my virginity list."

"Your virginity list?"

"It's what I call my bucket list. And I know that it sounds really bad after just faking an orgasm in the shower with our clothes on, but I just thought that, if you were willing, we could..."

And since he wouldn't shut up, I started to kiss him. And I mean that I kissed him. I kissed the boy I was falling in love with and hoped he would know that with that kiss I was giving him my heart.

And as the water was coming down on us, he put his arms around my waist and seemed to be enjoying the kiss. He was at least kissing me back as somebody that had some sort of feelings for me. It was loving and passionate, but not dirty or raw. It was beautiful.

And when I left him wanting more, I asked him, "Was it good for you?"

He slowly opened his eyes and in a drawn out way said, "Yeah. That's something I'm definitely going to be doing again." He then turned off the water and said, "We had better be going now."

And with our wet clothes on, we exited the bathroom. The drunk guy looked at us in amazement. Everybody else just looked at us as we left the party hand in hand. As I walked by Brittany, I held up my hand to show her the ring on my finger. I then flipped her off, which made me feel a whole lot better.

And then Jack and I walked home. It was a nice late summer evening. It was a perfect romantic evening where the stars were shining above and I was taking a leisurely stroll hand in hand with a guy that I liked. And we just talked as we made our way home.

He wouldn't tell me what other stuff was on his virginity list, but he did explain why he called it a virginity list. He said that if anything is worth doing once before you die, it should be amazing enough to want to do more than once. Plus, he said that you should have a list that you can mark off stuff with with some of the most important people in your life. He said that it makes it more special than just doing something because you want to. His list is stuff that he would like to do with other people.

So I took his kissing in the rain virginity. Although it was really his kissing in the shower virginity, I told him that I would officially pop his cherry the next time that it rained. He seemed to like that idea, so I must have been pretty good in conveying that I was starting to have feelings for him. I can't tell for sure.

When we got home, there was the question as to who should get in the shower first. He was going to be a gentleman and let me go first. I was going to be my typically slutty self and suggested that we should shower together again, except without clothes this time.

And he was nice about turning me down. He made sure that he was rejecting the idea and not actually rejecting me. He did it in such a way that I didn't feel like a slut, which I have been having problems with lately.

I'm going to have to remember that Jack just came out of a very long relationship. Having sex with a girl that he isn't actually dating probably isn't high on his list of priorities right now. Plus I have to be careful not to come off too strong in my feelings for him.

Anyway, we showered separately. Afterwards, we just hung out on the sofa watching TV. We did more talking than anything else. My guilty conscience got the better of me, and I asked him if he thought I was a slut.

The wisdom of asking a guy that you are interested in if he thinks you're a slut is probably not a good thing. I just wanted to get it out there for us to discuss. And in one of the more stupid things I have ever done with a guy, I ended up discussing almost my entire sexual history with him.

It was easy to do. Jack just held me, listened to me, and didn't judge me. I just wish I knew what he was thinking or feeling. It is making being in love with him hard for me. I don't want to ruin this, but I don't exactly know how to have a relationship with a guy that isn't ready for a relationship yet.

The Reasonable Woman Standard

By

Jack Webber

There are times in your life when the various sectors of your life come together to teach you important life lessons. This happened to me the other day at work as I was taking sexual harassment training. With a large portion of the sexual harassment taking place against women, the courts have decided to have a "reasonable woman standard" where a reasonable woman would determine whether something would be harassment or not.

Not to be offensive, but I have never found women to be very reasonable. This past weekend, I went to a party that I didn't really want to go to. I knew that I would be running into an ex-girlfriend that is currently dating my ex-best friend.

My date for the evening was a girl that knew everybody was going to be watching us as a couple, even though we aren't a real couple. Everybody knew that we weren't a real couple, and yet we still went to the party with the intent of putting on the greatest show on the earth.

A reasonable woman would have known that this would have turned out badly, which it did if you consider locking yourself in the bathroom and crying a bad thing. I think most reasonable women would define that as a disaster of the original plan of going to a party to make your ex jealous.

Of course, the reasonable man standard is not much better. I agreed to go to this predestined debacle with the full knowledge that it was going to be horrific. The difference between the reasonable man and the reasonable woman is that the reasonable man will agree to something that he knows he shouldn't do because a woman wants him to do it.

My reasons for going were that she wanted me to go, and I wanted to make her happy. Despite my objections and fears of impending doom, a reasonable man decided to just go with it. This was not done so that later I could say, "I told you so." My being right never entered into the equation. Somehow spending time with her and doing something with her that she wanted to do were my deciding factors. These are thoughts that any person would find reasonable.

The jury is still out on her reasons for wanting to go. Her argument was that we should get out of the house. Considering that we have spent most of our time together after the breakup of our previous relationship inside, going out to a party would be reasonable.

It would also be reasonable that she would want me to go to a party where I would get to see some of my male friends. I haven't seen them since this whole breakup thing happened. I have been rather isolated with my… girl that I'm spending my nights with and not having a real relationship with.

Okay. The jury just came back from deliberations. They have decided that she was a reasonable woman. This verdict was based on the facts that the man was found to be reasonable in agreeing to go to the party when he did so out of respect for and a desire to make the woman happy. Since both parties were thinking about somebody other than themselves, they are both deemed to be reasonable.

This, however, does not fully explain the woman in question's behavior the remainder of the night. It is reasonable that she would become upset when my ex-girlfriend implied that she was a slut. It is reasonable that she would lock herself in the bathroom at the party. Just like it is reasonable that I would pretend to be having sex with her in the bathroom. (There are times in your life where you find yourself in unusual situations and you have to improvise on what normal behavior would constitute. Faking sex in the shower to cover up for another person's crying due to being insulted is reasonable in this context.)

What becomes troubling behavior to understand is how the woman whose virtue came into question started to give a detailed history of her previous sex partners. Granted that a reasonable man is not dating this woman, she would have no reason to withhold this information from him. Both parties know that they are using each other for their own romantic rehabilitation.

In this instance, it seems like the woman sees the man as a close friend. Her sharing then would be seen as a way of discussing what is really bothering her and why she does the things that she does.

A reasonable man in this case would see the woman as a person that longs for love and has looked for it with the faith of a child. She gave her previous lovers all of her heart, and they refused to recognize just what they held in their hands. Throughout it all, she never gave up her faith in love and being loved.

She was a reasonable woman. She just never figured that men would never be able to see what she was offering.

The tragedy of the situation is that the reasonable man and the reasonable woman will continue to be reasonable and do everything that is in the best interest of the other person and then part ways, wishing each other the best of luck with their newly mended hearts in a world where such hearts cannot exist long.

I Saw Her Again Last Night II

By

Jack Webber

When going through romantic rehabilitation, there is always a choice that one has to make. Should you see your ex that you are trying to get over, or do you avoid them? The right answer to this question depends on the situation and the person. Seeing your ex could lead you back into temptation and long for the so called "golden days." On the other hand, seeing them might also prove that you have moved on and feel nothing for them.

I have no idea how I am actually doing in the rehabilitation process. A self audit is not high on my list of priorities at this time. To look at how I am coping with everything would just draw attention to the very thing that I am trying to forget and move on from.

When I saw her last night, I didn't feel the intense feelings of longing that I had even as recent as last week. She seemed more like a stranger that I knew extremely well. This made the confrontation awkward. Knowing your enemy intimately makes you go for the lowest of blows in order to achieve a decisive victory.

I should have wanted a victory in the same sense that she did, but my few remaining feelings for her kept me doing this. I merely finished the confrontation. I wasn't interested in a victor and a defeated the way that she was.

Knowing the "enemy" the way that I do, I was a little taken aback by her behavior. Considering that I was the one that was cheated on, I don't know why she would care who I spend time with after the breakup. But she is an extremely self-conscious woman, who has never thought of herself as beautiful. It didn't matter that I would tell her that I thought she was the most beautiful woman in the world. She never once found herself to be even remotely attractive.

I know that her attacks on my date were a defensive attack caused by her own insecurities. It meant that she thought that the woman that replaced her was superior in many ways. It also means that she is starting to doubt her decision to admit to the affair. She sees herself as a downgrade from the woman that she replaced.

If I were still madly in love with her, I would have told her that she didn't need to compare herself to other women. I would have told her that she was beautiful. And I might have cared that a beautiful woman didn't have any measure of self-worth.

Instead I found this woman that I knew so well to be horrifically ugly. When she said, "My God, Jack, you don't just give a diamond ring to the first girl that will fuck you", I couldn't help but to respond, "That girl has shown me more kindness than you did in four years, and you have just shown that she has more style, grace, and beauty than you could ever hope to have."

And that seemed to be the end of the confrontation. I left to comfort a woman that was deeply hurt by having her virtue challenged by a known cheater. By comforting my date, I found a beauty that I thought only my ex possessed. This new beauty seems more pure in its longing to be loved, desired, and appreciated for who she really is.

Despite having a night of discovering something that I once thought existed in my ex, I was still haunted by my former love later that night. She taunted me in my sleep and made me question that I would ever find somebody to replace her. She reminded me of the great things that we once were. She told me that she still cared for me. And when I confronted this ghost of my dreams about the fact that she was the one that left me, she said, "What could I do, Jack? You were killing me and our relationship. I had to leave. If I cheated, it was because I needed out and didn't want to hurt you."

And knowing her the way that I do, I almost believed these words. She would have told me these things and placed the blame on me for her cheating on me. And I couldn't argue with her.

Maybe I am to blame. Maybe I didn't love her enough, or expressed my feelings for her. Maybe I didn't make her feel that she was truly beautiful. If I had done these things, maybe she wouldn't have fallen for a man that could make her feel the things I never could in the four years that we were together.

Even though I know her words were not real and that she is dealing with her own feelings of insecurity after the breakup, I can't but help to believe that she would tell me these things if she wanted to cause me even more pain. Her respect for our previous relationship and what was once real has kept her from truly hurting me.

Instead, she will strike out at the person I am currently with. They are collateral damage. She doesn't care if they get hurt. I do. I don't want anybody else to feel what I have felt the past couple of weeks. I don't want anybody else to become a casualty of a failed relationship. If I have to suffer for the sake of others and deal with her ghost on a nightly basis, I am willing to do that. Nobody else will get hurt because of me.

Sept. 24, 2010

Jack has been different this week. He still has his moments of melancholy where he is silent and lost in thought, but he has also been more outgoing and wanting to do things. He has been seeing his friends and talking to them.

Tonight, Jack and I went to the movies. It was kind of a date. I don't want to officially call it a date, especially since Megan has been getting on to me about trying to read too much into everything I do with Jack.

Anyway, the other night, Jack and I were in bed. He has his left arm around me and he's playing with my hair with his right hand. We were just talking about stuff like we do, and then he goes, "What are you doing Friday night?"

I was caught a little off guard, but I told him that I didn't know.

He then said, "Well, I would like to take you out to a dinner and a movie... if you don't have other plans."

He seemed kind of nervous and acted like I was going to say no. He was really cute, actually.

I made sure that I didn't use the word "date" all week with him. I didn't want him to think that I thought we were dating and scare him off. Taking me out to dinner and a movie on a Friday night could mean something else to him than what I would like to think that it means, so I just had to find other ways to define it. We were two friends of the opposite sex spending time alone together where the man agreed to pay for everything and the man asked if I wanted to do this with him.

So despite this being the technical definition of date, I did not call it a date and neither did Jack. And maybe I don't really care about defining what tonight was. It was nice to get out of the house and to spend time with him.

He seemed to be a different person tonight when we were out. It wasn't like a Jekyll/Hyde thing or him having different moods as he is dealing with the breakup. And I can't really define what was different about him tonight.

He was sweet, kind, and caring, but he is usually that with me. He seemed interested in what I was saying, but he has always done that, even when we didn't really know each other. So I can't really say what was different, especially at dinner.

Dinner was at the local Italian place, which happens to be my favorite restaurant. He had been asking me questions all week trying to figure some place to take me. I wasn't going to tell him where I liked to eat in town. I didn't want him to try to treat me to a perfect date when I was pretty sure that he wasn't considering this a date. It would hurt too much later to know that everything that I thought was perfect was just to make me happy and not done out of any sort of feelings for me.

Anyway, he was able to figure out my favorite restaurant. He even made us reservations. And it was just a perfect dinner that I would have killed to have with any guy that I was dating, but there I was with a guy that I'm crazy about and not actually dating.

And I can't say what was different about him at dinner. Maybe it was just that he was out of the house. I think he is feeling a bit trapped in there all of the time. It's our safe place where we are free to make out with each other, discuss our deepest thoughts, fears, regrets, etc. To go out in public together and to know that people can see us and possible overhear something that we could say might have altered the way he acted with me tonight. But it wasn't like we were putting on a show like we did last weekend at the party.

After dinner, we walked around the mall for a little bit before going to the movies. At one point, he took my hand. He didn't just do that guy trick of testing the waters by accidentally bumping his hand into mine as we were walking. He made a clear decision to hold my hand, and yet it was completely natural and didn't feel like a guy putting the moves on me.

I don't want to say that he was putting the moves on me. I don't know that he was or ever has. When I smiled at him as he took my hand, he said, "I need to hold onto you. You're all I've got right now." It was extremely cheesy, but it was also very sweet and heartfelt.

It felt good to hold hands with him. I haven't done that with a guy in a very long time. I don't know why. I haven't been holding hands with the majority of the guys that I've dated lately.

It seems that the more intimate I have become with men physically, the less intimate I have become with men emotionally. That is the thing that I am finding about being with Jack. I'm okay with us not fooling around or having sex because I am spending so much more time getting to actually know him. And he does things like holding my hand, or holding me as we are talking.

Maybe he thinks of me as just a friend that is helping him to get over a breakup, but it feels nice to actually be a part of somebody's life and to be needed and wanted for something other than my sexual skills.

And it was nice to be on an actual date tonight with him where the guy paid for the dinner and movie. It was a simple date, but I haven't had a really nice date like tonight since a long time before Steve.

Maybe guys have changed from what I remembered wanting from them as I was growing up. Maybe I just accepted the reality of what men were like instead of demanding my expectations from them. Either way, I had a really good time tonight with Jack. I was able to watch the movie with him, and not have him try to make out with me throughout the film. He did play with my fingers in a cute, loving way during the movie, but it was more of that emotional connection kind of way than in the physical getting off sort of way.

It was just such a perfect date that I forgot that he was living with me. We were standing at the front door. We were holding hands and facing each other. I told him that I had a really great time tonight and then went in for that perfect kiss to top off the evening.

The kiss was amazing. I don't want to read something into it, but I think he put his feelings into it, too. And then there was this awkward moment where I didn't know what he was wanting, so I just smiled.

He then seemed a little sheepish and asked, "Do you have your key? I mean, I like kissing you out here and all, but the neighbors are kind of looking at us."

And then I remembered that I was living with the guy that I had just had the best first date of my life with.

There's not really a good way to recover from a situation like this, at least not gracefully where you don't give away that you like this guy. I ended up just apologizing, taking out my key, and then dropping my key. I started to bend over to pick it up, but then eyes caught a glimpse of his crotch, which looked nice in his jeans. And then I thought that bending over so that my head was in his general crotch area wasn't a good idea, so I said, "Can you pick that up for me? All I can think about right now is giving you a blowjob."

And as soon as I said it, I realized just how bad it sounded. And there was a moment where I contemplated whether I should try clarifying that statement by what I really meant to say, or whether the clarification would come out even worse than the original statement. But thinking that what I said was pretty bad, I decided to blabber out a clarification.

"Not that I'm mentally obsessed about giving you a blowjob right now. I just meant that I thought it might be awkward for me to bend over right now with you positioned the way you are to pick up the key. That's all I meant by saying that I was thinking about blowing you right now."

Which I then felt that my clarification needed a clarification. I didn't want to leave him with the impression that I was opposed to pleasuring him in that way. Ideally it would lead to him pleasuring me, which I would like very much. And it was out of that desire that I started to issue my clarification.

Thankfully before I got too far into this clarification, he had picked up the key, pulled me closer to him, and started to kiss me while opening the door. He then just gently led me inside and closed the door behind us. His kiss was soft and sweet. It wasn't like a guy leading me back to the bedroom, especially after I had initiated a conversation about blowjobs. And that is what kind of threw me off. So when I opened up my eyes and saw that beautiful face of his, I didn't quite know what to expect.

I certainly didn't expect him to say, "So is it okay if I call you sometime so that we can go out again?"

"I would like that very much."

I'm not going to read too much into him ending it like an official date. I think he was just trying to get me past the awkwardness of everything that I had just said, which makes him just a little bit cuter than what I already thought he was.

He then kissed me on the cheek and whispered in my ear, "I'm going to get ready for bed. I'll see you there later, but Megan is kind of looking at us like she is wanting to talk to you."

So Jack went to bed, and I went into the living room to talk to my best friend, whether it was to get a lecture or to share all of the details of the night's activities. It ended up being okay. She wasn't lecturing me. She just wanted to know what was happening between me and Jack, especially after she saw the way that we entered the apartment.

I told her that the kiss wasn't really what it seemed and explained the whole ~~date~~ evening with him. And when I got to the part about the blowjob outside, I mean, the discussion about the... Anyway, when I described the events leading up to his graceful exiting of my awkward moment, she understood what she saw a little bit better. But she did wonder whether he felt anything for me, or what was going on between us.

And I didn't know what to tell her. Not having ever dated a nice guy before, I don't know how to exactly take most of what Jack does. And it makes it harder in that we have this agreement where we are just using each other to get over a broken heart.

What confuses me the most is that he seems reluctant to be intimate with me. He seems comfortable holding me, kissing me, playing with my hair, and caressing me, but he has never tried to touch any of my sexual parts. I've just never been with a guy that didn't at least try to cop a feel by this point in our relationship, I mean, at this point in the amount of time that I have spent with him.

I don't know if when he touches me and kisses me that he is thinking about her, and that he won't do other sexual things because he knows that I'm not her. And I would ask him, but there is no good way to bring up something like this.

Besides, maybe it doesn't matter. I know that he is going through a hard time right now. And I am truly thankful to have him in my life right now. He makes me feel... like I have never felt before when I was with a guy. The actual definition of our relationship is relatively unimportant in that context.

When I made it to bed later that night, I found him lying there peacefully. He looked really beautiful with his arm flung up over his head. He looked like he wanted to be there and belonged there. And I would have stayed there admiring him, but I felt that was a bit creepy. So I tried my best to get into bed without disturbing him.

And I thought I had done a really great job of that when he rolled over on his side and put his arm around me. "You know, if I'm going to call you, you're going to have to give me your number."

I can't tell you how happy it made me that he said that to me. Although, considering that we have been sleeping together for three weeks now, it seems like we should have given each other our numbers before this. I tried to act like it wasn't a big deal, though. I figured this was the best thing to do since he had already started to cup my hand into his, playing with my fingers, and scooted closer so that he could spoon me, which gave away his hard on. I know guys can get those for any number of reasons, but I would like to think it was me and that he had been nursing one for as long as I was out there talking to Megan.

Anyway, I said, "Has not having my number been keeping you up all night?"

"No, not having you in my arms did that."

And there was really nothing to say to that. I mean, I wanted to let out a giant "Oooooh" sound that would convey just how cute that was, but it's generally best not to do that to in front of a guy. They don't like to know when they are being really cute and adorable. They think it makes them less of a man.

And I would have rolled over so that I could see him and make out with him, but I kind of wanted to wait and see what he was going to do. I didn't want to encourage him physically after I had made the blowjob comment earlier that night. It would be like rewarding his cuteness with a sexual favor. I felt like that was bad at this point in the relationship.

And yet I couldn't not respond to what he just said. If I didn't say anything, then he might take that to mean that I wasn't interested. So I had to think of something to say that would show that I was interested, but not overly interested. This somehow came out as, "If we had met at a bar or somewhere other than through

Steve, would you have still asked me out tonight?"

And he was quiet for a minute, as my heart was breaking for an answer and I was silently praying that he had somehow fallen asleep. He then said, "When was the last time a guy actually took you out on a date?"

And instead of answering the question, I ended up babbling on about meeting guys at parties or at the bar and doing more hooking up than dating. Even the dates I had had seemed less like a date and more like the formal trappings of a date with a guy that I was actually in a relationship with, even though I knew very little about the man, except what he looked like naked.

And when I had finally shut up and stopped revealing even more of my slutty past, he said, "You know, I'm still going to need your number. I generally like to call a girl the next day."

"We appreciate that. It keeps us from thinking that you're not going to call."

At that he just held me a little bit closer to him, and I was okay with him not saying anything. And before he fell asleep, I said, "And, Jack, you still haven't added me as a friend on FaceBook."

"I'll add you first thing in the morning."

"You don't need to worry about a relationship status between us. I would rather be listed as your friend than to be complicated with you or in an open relationship with you."

And that was the last thing that was said before we drifted off with me in his arms. And it was the most perfect first date I have ever had.

Two Lovers

By

Jack Webber

I've always considered myself an extremely faithful, one woman at a time man, but lately the strings of my heart have been being pulled in two different directions by two different women. It is making the whole romantic rehabilitation thing extremely difficult as I am trying to get over a confused thinking process that is now getting clouded by a confused heart.

Since the breakup with my ex, I am beginning to see that she was not the ideal woman that I have sometimes imagined her to be. Love polluted my vision of her. I have realized that especially lately, and this has nothing to do with her cheating on me. The cheating was like a spring thaw that awakened me from the winter I had grown accustomed to, but it was not something that I would call a character defect.

No, my realization of her true character came about after the breakup. When she attacked the woman that I am currently with for the appearance of any sort of promiscuous past she might have had, I started to realize that the woman I used to love was not what I had always thought that she was. And it made me realize that throughout my relationship with her that she engaged in this type of behavior.

I don't know how many times I have heard things like, "Did you see what she was wearing? Oh, my God! Look at her hair. Does she even own a mirror? Oh, look. She's with another guy this week. I guess looks and a slutty attitude are everything."

And I didn't think about it at the time, but she was always putting everybody else down and judging them on some sort of cultural concept and moral high ground that she seemed to possess. And I didn't think about her moral superiority in these matters. I could see where she was coming from in a purely societal sense. Some of these girls did have clothes that were horrendous, hair that looked awful, and were seen with a lot of men.

And since I have gotten to know the latest victim of her attacks, I have to say that the validity of the attacks may need to be revisited. Over the past two weeks, Liselle has shared her entire sexual history with me. Instead of judging her, I am finding myself wanting to be with her. There is an openness to her that longs to share herself with you. And instead of closing up like a hurt flower, she has always decided to continue to bloom and to share her beauty with the world.

If blooming meant that she got hurt in her pursuit of true love, she was willing to do that. And I respect that more than somebody that closes themselves off to the world and the chance of love. Instead of seeing herself as a victim of the game of love, she looks at each guy as a learning experience.

My ex, on the other hand, seems intent on some sort of moralistic crusade against love. The appearance of love is very important to her. And I fit that role for a very long time. I'm not sure what caused it to change, except that the concept of love can never compete with actual love. So when a relationship becomes stale and complacent, one of the people involved looks to alternate avenues.

And that leaves me. I don't know what I did wrong, or if I could have even done anything differently to have avoided the breakup. And as much as I am hurt and want to hate my ex, I am still partly in love with her. And I am finding a substitute lover in Liselle, which is not really fair to her.

When I am with Liselle, I have started to find a lot of what I missed when I was in a relationship. There's the physical touch of holding somebody in your arms, kissing them and having them kiss you back, and holding hands with somebody where you feel connected with something in this world.

I'm on shaky ground now when it comes to love. I know that I'm going through a certain amount of detox when it comes to my ex, but I'm afraid that I'm just replacing one drug for another. And I don't want Liselle to get hurt in the process. I want her close to me, and yet I know that I shouldn't. We both promised that we would just use each other to get over the breakup. When we are complete individuals, we will float on to our next lovers.

I wish I could tell you how the rehab was going. There are times when I hold Liselle and wish that it could be my ex. These times are getting fewer and farther between. Liselle did a good job in the beginning of trying to draw the poison from the years I spent with my ex, but lately she seems to be employing a new tactic in the rehab process. She has been breaking my already broken heart.

It was one thing to have my heart broken by being rejected as I was proposing to the supposed love of my life. It is quite another to have it broken by the physician treating me with her tales of past relationships. Maybe my heart was broken in a way that couldn't be mended the first time. It had to be rebroken and put into a cast.

I just hope that I don't end up hurting the doctor treating me. If I had been whole when I met her, or not poisoned by my previous relationship, I could have been perfect for her. Repaying one of the greatest friends I have ever had and one of the kindest people I have ever known with being another man in a line of regrets is not something that I want to do. I just don't know if I can overcome the toxins and grow my heart in time while it is confined in the cast of my past.

The Call

By

Jack Webber

There are some things that should be easy, like calling a girl that you've been living with for the past three weeks. But as I found myself on the phone with her for the first time, I discovered that the conversation that flowed freely every time that we talked started to get damned up somewhere in my mouth (although it could be my mind or heart that was damned as well).

> "Hi. I'm sorry for calling you so late, but I wanted to wait until I could find a good time to call you, which was kind of hard since I was with you all day today. I would have gone off into the other room to call you, but I figured that would look bad, even though I know you were expecting me to call you."
>
> *"It's okay. I'm glad you called. When are you coming to bed?"*
>
> "I will be there later. I just wanted to take this time to actually talk to you without being in bed with you."
>
> *"I accepted your friend request today. Thanks for sending that."*

"You're welcome. I, um… What are you doing next weekend? I know that it's a long ways off, but I wanted to see if you would want to go out again next weekend."

"You could ask me this in bed. You don't need to do it over the phone."

"I know, but I'm trying to wean myself off of your shelter. And I…"

And the fact of the matter is that I am a little confused right now. I know that I am feeling things that are similar to everything I was accustomed to with Brittney. I don't know if it is because I am using you as a substitute for everything that I miss about her, or if it is because I am feeling something for you. You see, that's the trouble with love. It feels good in the beginning, whether it is real or not. It takes time to prove that it has substance.

"…And I want to prove that I can actually have a conversation with you, without your look, touch, and embrace clouding my thinking."

"So what do you want to talk about? How my day was?

"No, I… Was your day okay?"

"It was glorious. Was it good for you?"

"It was… Do you have to make fun of me? I haven't gotten a girl's number in over four years, so I am kind of new to this."

"I'm not making fun of you. I think you're being really cute right now. I can't wait to tell Megan about this in the morning."

"Please, don't. What have you told her about me?"

"I can't tell you, but she is wondering what is happening between us. She's wanting me to put a label on it."

"You could tell her that we are FaceBook friends without benefits, but that you quite clearly want to give me a blowjob."

"I'm sorry. I'm going through a tunnel. I think I'm losing reception. You're breaking up."

"Well, before I lose you, could you answer my question about next weekend?"

"If you can answer my question about next weekend. Are you considering this a date?"

A date? A date by definition shows some sort of interest in pursuing a relationship with somebody else. I have spent the past few weeks in an isolated microcosm with this woman. As much as I have come to depend on her for everything, I know that love is a gamble that I may not be ready for. My answer would be a bet as I play a game of chance. That's another problem with love. Every good gambler knows there's a time to bluff and a time to show your cards.

"I consider last night a date."

"In that case, I will make sure that I don't forget to invite you in next weekend."

I have never been much of a gambler. I always enjoyed playing the game more than winning, but at least I had a game plan and never bet more than I could lose. When it comes to love, I don't know whether I'm bluffing or showing my cards right now. So I can't say if she is calling my bluff or not. Either way, I'm kind of down on my chips right now and will just enjoy seeing how the next few hands play out.

Sept. 26, 2010

So Jack has clarified that the other night was a date. The only problem now is that it still leaves us without a definition. We aren't hanging out, which is a good thing. That always means that a guy likes fooling around with you while he is trying to decide if he thinks of you in more than sexual terms.

Anyway, Jack still hasn't tried anything sexual with me, even after the whole blowjob comment. It's kind of nice being with a guy that I don't have to worry about groping me. It's also nice to not have a guy ask you to service him without being pleasured yourself. A lot of guys today expect you to blow them before they enter into a relationship with you. It's become as normal as kissing a guy.

When I was growing up, I always thought dating would be different than it turned out. You see stuff in movies or read about love in books, and it always seemed to be nicer than what it is in real life. And I'm not talking about that fairy tale sort of stuff that you see when you are kid where the guy is a prince and everything. I'm talking about soap operas, teen dramas, and Lifetime movies. They all make you think that really hot guys can be somewhat decent. And any drama they might pull is really just to make you interested in the story and to make you wait for the hot guy to realize that he is madly in love with the girl that he screwed things up with, which really just makes you want him more.

But in real life, I am finding that the really hot guys act like there are a lot of other girls that they could get, so they don't really have to treat you as anything special. And no matter how attractive you might be, you can always look around and see some girl that you know is better looking than you are.

And I don't want to blame some of my previous behavior on guys understanding that women are competing to be with them. I mean, part of my past actions have been because I did like the guy (if only physically). But after blowjobs on the first date and sex on the third date, I am finding that it hasn't exactly been good for developing a lasting relationship. It has led to some extraordinary sexual encounters, but that has never gone on to anything more enduring.

But, anyway, back to the relationship status thing with Jack. I don't think Jack and I are dating. He has asked me on dates, but this doesn't seem to be dating in the classical sense. Of course, in the classical sense of the word, the couple isn't living together as they start their relationship. So given our circumstances, some things are going to be messed up, which I kind of regret now considering that I probably could have had a perfect relationship with him if we would have met and gotten together in a different way.

I'm hoping that the definitions get clarified when we reach that "in a relationship" stage. It's just that with hanging out, talking to, dating, and going out with guys nowadays that things have gotten very confusing. You don't know what you are doing with them, or what they are feeling for you. And you don't want to get too involved emotionally until you are sure that the guy feels the same way. If you start to feel too much, you are just setting yourself up for heartache. And yet, if you don't allow yourself to feel anything for the guy, then you end just having sex with them, which doesn't exactly work out either.

And if things were normal between me and Jack like a relationship should be, then I would have the "Where do you see us going" talk with him, which I kind of want to do right now. It's not so much that I am concerned about a relationship status. I feel like we need to have the sex talk, which I haven't had with a guy since James Michael Finch in high school. And that conversation took place three months and many blue balls for James before we actually had sex.

And I don't know why I haven't had the sex talk with any guy after that. I guess I just kind of went with the flow with everybody else. I told a few guys to stop a few times, but then I usually ended up having sex with them a couple of weeks later.

I guess alcohol played a certain role in some of my sexual decisions with guys I was seeing. And once you have sex with a guy that you are kind of seeing, dating, or whatever, it is a lot easier to keep having sex with him. You almost feel more for him than that physical attraction stuff. You do actually care for him like you do when you are in a committed and caring relationship. And the guy is actually more attentive to you. You know that they are no longer with you just to get some. So getting the sex out of the way has its certain benefits, if only for a short period of time.

Eventually the sex doesn't become enough to sustain the relationship. You start to see that even really hot guys have physical faults as well as severe personality defects. Even if you try to recapture the magic that existed in the beginning, you realize that it was never real to begin with. And you wonder what happened and how your opinion could change so much in as little as two or three months.

Anyway, this is the longest I have gone without sex since I have become sexually active. It's not that I'm missing the act right now. I think I probably should somehow. I mean, I usually hook up with a guy right after I break up with somebody.

That's the odd thing about this whole thing with Jack. I don't feel like I'm a totally unlovable person, which is how I usually feel right after a break up.

In terms of actually be successful, I think this whole rehab thing is working. I've changed a lot of my previous negative behavior and am engaging in truly positive things. I just don't know if I had a sex talk with Jack if it would screw up everything and count as a setback.

The Talk

By
Jack Webber

There are times in my life where I wonder how I came to be in the situation that I am in. They seem to be so absurd that you would think you were in the middle of a comedy, and yet you recognize it as your real life.

I had a moment like this the other day when I was in bed with Liselle. She turned to me and said, "So about that blowjob?"

She said it with such frankness and sincerity that I knew I was in for an interesting discussion to say the least. But there is very little that you can say after that, except, "Yes?"

"I was thinking... Not that I'm dying to give you a blowjob... I mean, I'm not obsessed with giving you one, but if you wanted me to, I'm not opposed to it."

"Um, okay. I, uh, like you a lot and feel really uncomfortable with you doing that to me. Not that I am opposed to you as a person doing that. I just didn't really give your comment the other day much thought."

"Are you rejecting me?"

"No! No. I'm just not accepting… I mean, I have never really been one of those guys that has enjoyed that sort of thing. It's not you. It's me."

Even when refusing a blowjob, it is best to never tell a girl that it is you and not her. I'm guessing this is the case based on the look on her face. That's the only experience I have with telling a girl that it is me and not her in a situation like this. I'm not sure how often these situations come up, but I figured that it is better for you to be more prepared for it than I was.

"It's really not you. I have serious issues. The idea of you… Look, I know where my dick has been. Not that it has been any places that I would be ashamed of, or afraid to admit to you. I just… The idea of you doing that to me with your mouth when I would then be kissing you, kind of bothers me. So you see it really is me and not you."

And she was speechless for a moment. I don't know if she was trying to process my explanation as something believable, or if she thought that I was totally insane. There is a very fine line with how much you should reveal to a girl that you just getting to know.

"So you're never going to ask me to…?"

"No, there's the whole me wanting to kiss you thing, and I think it is kind of rude for me to ask you to brush your teeth and use mouthwash after doing something like that. Plus, I just… Okay, I've seen the videos online, and I just don't get it."

"You don't get women giving men pleasure?"

"Oh, I get that, but I'm like… Okay. So the guy is either really passive, or he's almost brutal in shoving something in another human being's face. It's just not what I look for in a sex act."

"And what do you look for in a sex act?"

"Mutual satisfaction where both people are treated with respect and dignity."

"So…"

"Are we having the "sex" talk?"

"No."

The amazing thing about women is that they will deny the truth while continuing their line of questioning that affirms everything that they are denying.

"No, I just thought that, well, I haven't been with a guy since Steve, and since we are supposed to use each other."

"You're wondering when I'm going to fill the void left by him?"

"No, I..."

The sex talk is one of the most awkward talks you will ever have with a woman. It's not awkward in the way that it was with your parents when you were a teen. Instead of talking about the mechanics of sex and the consequences and moral issues involved, the sex talk with a potential partner is more of a listing of sex acts that you are comfortable performing or having performed on you. It's a negotiation process.

"I really like you, Liselle. There's a part of me that wants to have sex with you. It's mainly my penis, but there's a smaller section of my heart that is willing to go along with it. It's just that the rest of my heart and a good portion of my brain is telling me to be careful and not hurt you."
"So it's not..."

"It's not you. It's me. You're a very beautiful girl. If we had met under other circumstances, and if I was the type of guy that could just use somebody, I would totally be trying to do you right now."

And as awkward as I was at that moment, her pure smile made me know that I was on the right road.

"So what are we exactly?"

The amazing thing about women is that they can go from wanting to just have sex with you to wanting to define your relationship to them.

"I don't know. I'm a little bit messed up right now. So, as your friend, I would probably tell you not to date me right now."

"But there's a part of your penis and your heart that want to make love to me?"

"It's more the penis with a small section of the heart, but, in all honesty, my heart is not something that I exactly trust right now."

"And what about your head?"

"It's trying to be rational with physical and emotional appeals to its intellect."

"So?"

"So, if you need sexual satisfaction, my feelings wouldn't be hurt if you used a vibrator."

"And if I need more than just sexual satisfaction from the man I'm sharing my bed with?"

"Then you might need to find a new man to share it with. I'm giving you all that I have."

And as hard as it was for me to say, it was even harder to watch her spirit fall after I said it. And even though I knew her heart was breaking, I was really glad that she kissed me. I needed that.

I can almost see me giving her my heart, so that she can rebuild it to be what she needs it to be. I just don't know if she can rebuild it in time to be of any use to her.

Oct. 2, 2010

Jack and I went out last night on our second date. He wouldn't tell me where we were going all week. He would only tell me that I should dress up. We had dinner at Cucino Di Betto.

I can't figure him out. He seems to be going back and forth on what he wants. Earlier this week, he was acting like he wasn't sure that he was willing to have relationship. And then last night, he took me to the best date restaurant in town.

And it wasn't just that he took me there and paid for dinner. He was... He was how I wished all of my other dates could have been. And it wasn't just that he treated me special by pulling my chair out and standing up when I went to the bathroom. It was how he couldn't take his eyes off of me all night.

And dinner was amazing. Instead of two friends out on a date, he was actually trying to get to know me as a lover. I could tell that he was trying to steer the conversation a certain way. It wasn't just talk about my major or people that we knew. It was about me as a person and what I want out of life. And it was about me.

After dinner, he took me to the art museum. We just walked around and discussed the paintings and sculptures. At first I thought it was an odd sort of place for a date, and then we started talking. It seems that he is getting a degree in Art History. He said that it was one of those crazy things you do in college.

I learned that he used to paint and make things. He still takes photographs and makes movies in addition to doing some writing. The Art History classes were just easy for him. He doesn't really want to go into that as a career or anything.

I asked him what the point of doing it was then. He kind of laughed to himself and said, "Sometimes I just need to have something beautiful in my life and to know that somebody else has felt the same things I'm feeling."

And as I walked around with him as my personal tour guide, I learned about him more than I did about the paintings. It's not that he wasn't knowledgeable. For the first time since we have been together, he seemed to open up to me.

I don't know if that is why he brought me here or not. A part of me thinks that he thought it would be a really great place to take a date. And part of me thinks that he took me there to see how I would respond to it. He said something about trying to take Brittany here and how she never seemed to enjoy it.

He breaks my heart. I could love him, and I think he wants to love me. He just won't deal with the ghost of his ex. Her memory seems to be around almost everything that we do.

After the museum, he took me to a little park in town. He had packed a few snacks and drinks in a picnic basket. We sat outside and looked at the stars and just talked. In a little bit, he pulled out some portable speakers and his MP3 player, and we danced under the stars.

I haven't slow danced with a guy since the eighth grade. I had forgotten how nice it was. I have gotten so used to guys gyrating on me that it made this feel all the more special. I can't quite explain it. This was somehow more intimate than even rubbing my ass against some guy's crotch.

And I don't know why, but as we were dancing, I asked him, "Do you always take girls out on dates like this?"

"Yeah. Well, I used to, and then Brittany seemed to get bored by them. Is there something wrong with dates like this?"

"No, they're absolutely perfect. You've given me the best dates I've ever been on." And as much as I tried to make it sound like I wasn't madly in love with him, I think I gave myself away.

"At what point do you think she got bored with me and was afraid to tell me?"

And I didn't know what to say, so I just kissed him. I don't know if he wanted me to at that moment, but he let me. And I don't know why, but I felt kind of guilty after having done it. Maybe it was because I haven't really kissed a guy that I've really liked in a very long time. I mean, I've kissed guys that I'm physically attracted to, but Jack has this sweetness and purity to him that makes him really attractive. And his love for Brittany makes him a guy that I can't have. It's like he's a sweet, forbidden fruit.

I felt really embarrassed after having kissed him. And I think he knew that it was not just a random kiss with a girl that he has kissed before. So I just put my head on his shoulder and continued to dance with him knowing that we weren't ever meant to be a couple and that I should enjoy this while it lasts.

And we danced in this odd, peaceful silence for I don't know how long before he said, "Liselle, my cousin is getting married next weekend. Are you free to go to the wedding with me?"

"I would love to."

And he held me closer as we continued to dance.

I'm not sure how long we danced or when we got home. Both of us seemed to be really relaxed when we got back to the apartment. There was just there serene silence over us where neither one of us talked, but it was okay.

And we managed to avoid the awkwardness of ending the date like we had last weekend. We just went inside and got ready to go to bed. I was in bed when he climbed in and kissed me on the forehead.

As I snuggled up to him and put my head on his chest, I noticed that he always wears a t-shirt to bed and that I've never seen him shirtless. And before I could stop myself, I said, "Is there a reason you always wear a shirt to bed?"

His response to that was just laughter.

"What's so funny about that?"

"Oh, nothing. It just seems that I can't take you out without you either wanting to give me a blowjob or take off my shirt", he said with very nice smile on his face. It was hard to be angry at him, especially when he is so cute when he smiles and is genuinely happy, especially when I am the one that made him happy.

"Fine. I don't want to see your six pack anyway", I said as I rolled over and ignored him.

That's when he put his arm around me and changed his tone. "Well, if you think I have a six pack, then you would be disappointed. Not that you wouldn't be disappointed anyway after having been with Steve. I know why Brittany left me for him."

I don't know how he can touch me so sweetly when he is talking so frankly about them. It's like there is a disconnect between what he says and what he's thinking and feeling.

"Do you really think she cheated on you because of your body?"

"Wouldn't you?"

"No. Women don't cheat on men that they've been in a relationship with that long just because of the guy's physical appearance."

He looked at me for a minute as he thought about what to say. He then sat up in bed and took off his shirt. And that's when it slipped out.

"Holy Fuck, you're hot."

He just shook his head and got out of bed. I don't know why, but he seemed to be upset about something.

"Do you have to make fun of me? I can look in the mirror and know that this isn't the ideal", he said. "And I've seen Steve shirtless. I know why girls would want to go out with him." And then he got really depressed as if remembering something, "And I've been shirtless around Brittany. She never reacted that way."

"So you're an expert on what women find attractive about men", I said as I got out of bed and made my way over to him.

"No... I just mean that...."

As I got closer to him, I think I was actually beginning to intimidate him. That's when I cornered him and pushed him down on the bed. Once I got him down, I started kissing his biceps.

"Your biceps are well defined, but not overly big. Girls want strong men, but not a guy that is going to spend all day at the gym and never see us."

As he was checking out his biceps, I made my way to his shoulders. "And your shoulders are just as equally defined. Natural looking and not overly developed, leaving you without a neck.

But where your body starts to really get amazing is at your chest. You have really nice pecks."

I looked at him as I massaged his pecks.

"You don't mind that I can't grow any type of hair there", was all he could say.

My response came after I kissed his chest and ended up licking his nipples. I stared him straight in the eyes and said, "No."

I then started to make my way down his stomach. "I mean, you have hair leading down to your goods. Who needs it on your chest?"

It was one thing to touch his defined abs with my hands. Using my tongue to go down the path his hair created was probably a bit too much. I just couldn't help myself. It's not very often that you get to actually tell a guy how good looking they are.

"And to top it all off, you have these sexy V lines, whose edges are just barely visible under your pants. It's a shame really. I would very much like to see those."

At that point, I just left him there speechless and got back into bed as if I didn't care. "Steve has nothing on you. And I don't know how Brittany was able to keep her hands off of you or was stupid enough to leave you."

I never expected him to say, "She never seemed interested in me. When she first starting spending the night, I used to go to bed without a shirt. She made fun of the few hairs I could grow on my chest. She told me I should take care of those few stragglers because they weren't very attractive. I then started to shave my chest, and she told me it was like going to bed with a thirteen year old boy instead of a guy in college."

Knowing that it wouldn't really comfort him, I said, "There's nothing wrong with your body. You're built like a swimmer. You're lean and sexy. And there's nothing wrong with the amount of body hair that you have."

"What was it then," he said with such a sadness that it almost broke my heart. "What was it about me that made her leave me and fall for Steve?"

"What makes it think that it was you at all?"

"Because I was with her for four years. During that time, she always pulled away from me physically. If I started to touch her in any way that I would have liked to, she asked me to stop and told me that she was saving herself for marriage. The last time I checked, she isn't married and is doing a lot of the things I wanted to do with her, except that she is doing them with Steve."

It was at this point that I started crying. I didn't mean to. And the more that I tried to stop, the more that I cried even more.

Jack tried to comfort me, but I don't think he knew exactly what was wrong. I think he thought he was the reason that I was crying, which made him want to make me stop crying and made me cry harder.

He finally ended up saying, "Do you want me to sleep on the couch tonight? I don't want to be making you cry all night."

At that point, I just got on top of him and started kissing him, which I think confused him even more. I could tell from his lips that he didn't really want to be kissing me, but he was also getting a massive erection.

"I wish I could love you", was all that he could say.

We spent the next few hours talking.

Brittany did a lot of damage to him. He feels guilty touching a woman other than her. Even if he wants to be sexual with me, she conditioned him that it was a sin.

At least I have some answers as to why he has never fondled me or treated me as a sex object. And he admitted to liking me, but said that it would probably be best if we didn't date. He says that he doesn't want to hurt me.

It's funny that guys always say that they don't want to hurt you when what they do ends up hurting you. At least, he was honest in saying that it wouldn't be fair to me to start a relationship with me.

Of all of the guys that I've dated, he's the one I've fallen the hardest for. Part of it has to be that he's the most decent man I've ever met. He's intelligent, fun to talk to, and he listens. Plus he wants me and refuses to actually go out with me. He's the first challenge I've had in a very long time.

The Dance

By
Jack Webber

If there is one thing I have learned about love is that it always seems extremely normal when you in the midst of it. It is only once the romance is over that you begin to see just how messed up everything was.

I had known Brittany for as long as I can remember. She had been in my classes in grade school. I didn't take much notice of her back then. In fact, we were casual friends for ten years. And then one day when I was a junior in high school, something changed. There was something about her that made me think of her in romantic terms.

Our love story started at a Home Coming Dance. I originally went to the dance with Jenny Warburton. We were just friends and went as such. She was fun to hang out with and easier to talk to about things I might be thinking or feeling than Steve was. In many ways, I see these qualities in Liselle now.

Anyway, Brittany had gone to the dance without a date. She was hanging out with a group of her female friends. I remember them being in a big group just giggling and dancing together. What I remember most about that night was the way that Brittany looked in her jade green dress. It was a silky dress that showed off her curves and revealed the beauty of her back.

In the midst of the group of giggling girls, she looked over at me. Our eyes met, and she bit her lower lip. I would later learn that this was a quirk of hers when she got nervous. And I don't know why, but I walked over to her with no idea of what I was even going to say to her.

When I got over to her, we both just looked at each other, and there was an extremely awkward silence that probably matched my actions. And with her friends staring at me and laughing, I somehow managed to stammer out, "Would you like to dance?"

Even today I can still remember how sweet her, "I would love to", sounded.

I don't remember what song we first danced to. The majority of my senses were dulled in her presence. All I can remember was the vision of loveliness that was dancing with me. I know that our first dance was a slow dance. I know that I liked the way that she felt in my arms. I know that I managed to stutter enough words together to tell her how beautiful she looked. Everything else was a blur at that particular moment in time for me, or I have forgotten it completely.

I do remember her asking me if I thought my date would get upset because I was dancing with her. I told her that Jenny and I were just friends. She tried to tell me that sometimes a girl is just friends with a guy when they really want more.

"Well, she's told me all of the guys that she has a crush on. I'm pretty sure we're just friends", I said as I gently caressed her bare back.

"And how long have you had a crush on me," she said with a smile playing on her lips.

"I… um… don't have a crush on you. I just saw you over there and wanted to be with you", was all that I could say.

I'm sure that it didn't come out the way that I wanted, but I didn't expect her to say, "And how much have you had to drink tonight?"

"I'm… um… completely sober. I'm just… naturally this awkward… and clumsy. I have no idea what I'm doing right now. I just saw you and haven't really done much thinking since then. Do I smell like alcohol? I tried aftershave today. I thought girls like that sort of thing, even if I put it on for a girl I'm just friends with."

This made her smile, and in a good way. "You smell very good." And so we danced without knowing how else to continue this conversation.

I don't know how long the silence raged before I finally broke it, or shattered it with my extreme awkwardness, "Am I dancing okay for you?"

"Excuse me?"

"I… uh… I haven't danced with that many girls, and well, the girls I have danced with were just friends, so I wasn't that concerned about… um… impressing them. So this is the first time in my life where I actually care if I'm… um…

somewhat decent at dancing, so that I can ask you out. Or hang out. I mean, we can hang out before actually going out on a date. I just want to get to know you… better. I would like to know more about you."

"Do you have your cell phone on you", she asked with a shy smile on her lips.

"Yes", I said as I fumbled around in my pocket to pull it out. "Actually that was the hard thing that rubbed next to you a minute ago."

And as she laughed at me, I became more embarrassed and tried to clarify it with, "I just didn't want you to think that I was some pervert wanting to dance with you so that I could…"

And it was at that point that I dropped my phone as I tried to open it. It fell under her dress. I thought that my chances with her were over. I stopped talking. I knew that my explanations were just making the situation worse.

To my surprise, she bent down and picked up my phone. She then went to my contacts and added her number.

When she handed me back my phone, she said, "Call me sometime. You can either ask me out or ask me to hang out."

And then she walked away. I watched the lovely flow of her dress and her beautiful form as she left me. I was lost in a moment until she turned around and said, "You'd better rejoin your friend. Even girls that you're just friends with don't like to be left alone at dances."

I went back to Jenny and was bombarded with questions about Brittany. I tried to answer them the best that I could, but it was just one dance. It has always amazed me that women can think of so many questions for an event that guys consider insignificant at the time. I don't know if women have some sort of extra sense that tells them that something is more important than what guys think it is.

Brittany and I didn't talk again for the rest of the night. We glanced over at each other, but that was it. I danced with Jenny and kept her company. She made me go over everything that happened with Brittany during the dance and told me how sweet it was.

I was sure that I had made a complete and utter fool of myself. Jenny just told me that I was really cute and that cute was a good thing.

I don't know. I still wasn't thinking. I wasn't even thinking when I called Brittany the next day. We ended up talking for half an hour before I finally asked her out. I asked her if she would like to do something next weekend. She then said that she wouldn't mind doing something tonight.

We ended up going to dinner and a movie that night. Everything just worked out. The conversation flowed freely. And I think we both knew that we would be a couple.

I never had to work on the relationship. Maybe that was the problem. With everything being so perfect and me never thinking about what I was doing, I became lazy and never realized that there were problems.

Maybe I became so confident in us as a couple that I forgot to tell her how beautiful she was. Maybe that is why she cheated on me. Steve has an innate ability to make women feel special. Being a natural flirt and the type of guy who never says no, he could have easily have flattered her. She then would have encouraged him knowing that he could give her things that I wasn't in our relationship.

Liselle can say what she wants about me, but I still think that I was to blame for the breakup.

Since the breakup with Brittany, I have thought about that dance on several occasions. I have wondered what would have happened if I had never asked her to dance. I could have saved myself the pain I have been experiencing the last month, but I would have missed one of the greatest experiences of my life.

When I danced with Liselle the other night, I thought about Brittany sometimes. That dance will forever haunt me as will Brittany. But then there were times when I thought of Liselle and how nice she looked, how I enjoyed being with her, and how I would not want to be dancing with anybody else right now.

Oct. 8, 2010

I went to the mall today and bought some lingerie. I'm not exactly sure why. Jack told me the other day that maybe it would be best if we didn't date. He doesn't think it is fair to me since he thinks that I'm starting to develop feelings for him and he is still in love with Brittany. So naturally I buy lingerie to entice him.

I decided to not go the extra slutty route. I didn't want to appear to be easy when I am throwing myself at a guy that doesn't really want me.

I can't say that he doesn't totally not want me. He has been coming to bed the past few nights without a shirt. It's like he's teasing me with his sexy body, which was just a little bit sexier by the fact that he felt a little shy being shirtless around me. It's nice to know that guys feel self-conscious about their bodies too. I didn't think they would since the majority of the guys I know are so eager to get naked with me.

Anyway, tonight when he came to bed, I had a bottle of men's body lotion and offered to give him a massage. I figured that it was the most intimate thing that I could do with him while still pretending to be just friends.

He didn't even put up a fight. All I had to do was tell him that I noticed his skin was getting a little dry last night. I assured him that it wasn't his fault. It happens this time of year. I then offered to rub it on him.

The thing I've noticed about Jack is that he seems to want to please people. There is a lack of confidence in him that seems to doubt everything about himself as if he is not worthy. I can't bring this up to him, though, without making him self-conscious about it. Anyway, I would rather have a guy that stops and thinks about what you think about them and what they're doing than to have a guy that's an asshole that does whatever he wants without thinking about you.

Anyway, I started the massage with his back. He has a really nice ass. I didn't get to see it or anything. I just felt how firm it was as I was straddling him massaging his back.

I felt that the best way to show that I was thinking about him and not just doing this as a way to seduce him was to have him tell me about Brittany and their relationship.

He told me about how they met. And it was a really cute story. I don't have any stories like that with any guy that I've dated. But what struck me the most was how he looks at love as chance happenings. He doesn't think you can plan it. It just sort of happens without any forethought of the people involved.

That's when I accidentally told him that I disagreed and that all of my experiences with love have been random hookups and not chance encounters that ever taught me anything meaningful.

I realized that this was a mistake as soon as he offered to give me a massage as I talked about my relationship issues. Fortunately I was able to keep this focused on him

I had him roll over so that he was now on his back. I then straddled him and started to massage the front of his shoulders and his pecks. I also rubbed the lotion over his abs. As much as he tried to hide it, I could tell that he was getting turned on.

And then there was that awkward moment where we were both looking at each other and nothing happened. I had no choice but to dismount and gracefully acknowledge, "Well, I think you are fully lotioned. We'll have to do this again tomorrow night."

As I settled into bed with him, I wondered to myself whether it was more painful to have him there beside me knowing that I could turn him on and not make him love me, or knowing that he was so unattracted to me that he hadn't even noticed the lingerie and the way that I had done my hair and makeup just for him.

And as much as it comforted me, it also hurt me when he cuddled up next to me and put his arm around me.

Then he whispered in my ear, "It's 11:11. Make a wish."

And I wished that I could keep myself from not totally breaking down and crying in front of him right now.

"Did you make a wish", he said as if he were a kid and believed that it could be true.

So I told him yes, kissed him, and told him that we couldn't share what we wished for or it wouldn't come true.

"I don't think there's any problem with that. I wished that we had met under different circumstances. If I don't make love to you, it's not because I don't want to, or don't think that you're extremely beautiful. I just don't want you to regret anything as we're trying to heal each other", he said.

"And what if we're supposed to be together and you're fighting chance?"

"Chance doesn't go to bed with her hair made up and makeup on."

"But what if you walked up to Brittany that night and had that dance all by chance to get you to me as I happened to be with Steve", I said. "What if every failed relationship I have had has led me to you so that I could help you learn how to express your sexual desires?"

"Help me learn to express my sexual desires?"

"Yes. You're sexologically stunted, and it's all because of her and her celibacy rules. How much did you want to do with her and were never allowed to do? She's made it so that you can't even touch a woman and not feel ashamed. That's not normal."

"And what? You want me to just simply use your body because you think I'm sexologically stunted", he said as he came in closer to me. "I'm sorry, Liselle, but love never comes at the expense of another. I'm not going to use you, or ask you to sacrifice yourself for me and my problems."

And as I rolled away from him, I started to cry. "The guy I lost my virginity to thought I could lose some weight. I dieted, and he thought I could still lose some weight. After that, I just started sleeping with guys because it was a way to get them to like me when I was surrounded by so many other prettier girls."

It was at this point that he started to actually touch me. "When I'm with you I want to do things with you that I've never wanted to do with Brittany, and it makes me feel ashamed because it makes me question what I had with her. But don't confuse my issues with your sex appeal and natural beauty."

And he kissed me with soft, sweet kisses. And as he gently dried my tears, we looked at each other. I don't know if I kissed him first or if he started it, but the kissing became heavier. And he soon took the lead.

I've had guys undress me many times before, but I've never had a guy want me naked so bad while still being gentle with me. His passion was tempered with a desire to please me in the process.

And I can't say that he did anything any different than any guy before him, except the care and attention that he was giving me. He seemed to really enjoy kissing my body, and not just my breasts.

This was actual foreplay and not some guy trying to get me naked so that we could have sex. And I don't know how long it lasted. I just know that Jack didn't stop, except when he got down to my underwear. He looked up at me, and I gave him the go ahead with my eyes.

I don't know what made it so amazing. Part of it was that he reached his hand up for me to take. And I liked running my fingers through his hair. More than just getting serviced by somebody that I liked, I felt emotionally connected to them as well as physically connected. I don't remember that ever happening before.

And I don't know if it was him, his technique, or the amount of time he devoted to the act, but I ended up squirting, which wouldn't have been so bad, except that since I had been playing with his hair, I kind of pulled his face right into it as it was happening.

He seemed to handle it okay. I was more than a little embarrassed. Before we could really talk about it, I wiped off his face with the sheets and told him to run through the shower while I cleaned up the bed.

After his shower, he came back into the bedroom. He was smelling really good and looking really hot. His hair was still a little wet and his chest was damp like he had just taken a really hot shower that made him perspire a little. And there I was in an old t-shirt and a pair of pajama bottoms waiting for him to start the conversation, which he did with, "You decided to get out of your lingerie?"

"I'm not exactly feeling sexy right now", I said with as much grace and dignity as I could.

That's when he got in bed next to me and put his arms around me. "Was that the first time that's happened?"

"Yeah. I'll try to make sure that it doesn't happen again. But I'll understand if you decide to not...", I said avoiding eye contact as much as I could.

He tilted my head up and made me look him in the eyes. "You didn't do anything wrong. And you may not believe it, but I'm glad that I was able to pleasure you in a way that Steve and other guys have not been able to."

He kissed me, and I knew that it was okay. And he just held me. There were things that I wanted to ask him, but I felt they were better left unsaid. So as I felt safe, secure, and loved within his arms I had to try to dismiss the thought of whether he was thinking of me or Brittany as he was getting me off.

Maybe it doesn't matter. He is making a lot of progress. I should be happy with that. He's no longer afraid to touch my breasts or to go down on me. Being with him makes me happy. And if I can heal him enough, I think I could make him happy, too.

I will see how he introduces me to people at the wedding since he has started to pull back from the whole dating thing. I can't really blame him for that, though. I have made it kind of awkward for us after the dates. I will have to remember to be less... me or whatever... at the wedding.

Damaged Goods
By
Jack Webber

Over the past week, Liselle and I have been trying to prepare ourselves as we get ready to debut our relationship to my family. As we have started to develop our official narrative, we have had to discuss the less than ideal way in which we came to know each other. As we have tried to write a socially acceptable story to tell people, I have started to realize just how damaged we are.

How are we going to say that we met?

You can lie and say that after Brittany cheated on you that you turned to me for comfort. Your family doesn't need to know that when we left the bar that night that we were planning on having sex.

I will say that you were the only person I could turn to with my sorrow. As we continued to talk and share our feelings about having been cheated on, we discovered that something more was there.

When you came home with me that night, were you planning on having sex with me?

I had thought about it. I wanted to do something to get back at Brittany. I wanted something to take the pain away. I'm glad now that I decided not to go through with it. I would have hated using you that way.

Don't worry about it. I've been used like that before, and I've used guys for that before.

Would you have really slept with me that night?

Yeah. That's why I invited you back to my place.

What did you think of me that night? Did you feel anything for me?

I felt sorry for you.

So it would have been a pity fuck?

No. You broke my heart that night. I saw a man that was experiencing a lot of the same things that I had gone through before when some of my relationships had ended. Since you had always been nice to me, I thought I would see what I could do to help you. I figured that it would be better if I was the one that got used by you, instead of somebody else. At least I would understand where your heartache was coming from. And I wouldn't judge you for not calling me the next day.

Why did you agree to let me stay with you?

You were really sweet. And you broke my heart. And you needed me. Then when you suggested that we use each other to get over the heartache, I thought of how nice that it would. It saved me from a random hookup with a guy that was just going to be using me.

So that was it? There wasn't anything special about me?

No. I mean, you were... When I told Megan that you were going to be staying with me, she said that I made you sound like a puppy that I had found on the streets and was trying to keep.

A puppy?

I know that it doesn't sound good, but... A lot of times when I have tried to use men, I have gotten hurt even more. They were just a man trying to fill the role of something that I needed, but they never did. And then, here you were, this cute, little, heartbroken, puppy of a man that needed me. And it felt good to be needed and to have a man that was pretty drunk still have the wits about him to say no to me when I offered to sleep with him.

A puppy, huh?

Yeah, but what surprised me the most was the fact that you were potty trained. Of all of the drunk guys I've gone home with, you were the first one that didn't piss on me in the middle of the night.

Does that happen a lot?

You'd be surprised. So when I say that you were a cute, little puppy that needed me, I mean it as a girl that has gone home with guys with the promise of food, shelter, and love. You were the male version of me. I couldn't leave something like that out on the streets.

In many ways, it bothers me to have her talk about the number of guys that she's been with. It's not the actual number, and I don't care about the number, even if I do eventually end up making love to her at some point in the future. What bothers me is that she can just so freely admit to having sex with guys that she didn't care about.

And with her admissions comes a sorrow as if that was all that she deserved. I would almost say that she isn't ashamed, but it's not that. She knows that she can't change the past. She has no desire to. She made her decisions, seems to know that they were poor and things that she wouldn't do now, but she talks about them openly as if she is begging you to love her for who she really is.

She wants somebody to love her. Guys have made love to her, but they have never loved her. And as I think of Steve and what he used to tell me about her, I see that he missed so much of who she is as an individual.

I like that she thought of me as a puppy the night that Brittany left me. I imagine that I did look like something that you would see in those SPCA commercials where they show you images of animals that have been mistreated as a sad song plays and a celebrity asks you to help.

We're both damaged goods. Animals that only wanted to be loved and cared for by the people we tried to be devoted to. In the end, we were mistreated and have been trying to cope with the wrongs done to us as if it was something that we did.

If I were ever truly honest with myself, I would admit that I love her. I love how she makes me feel, how she is totally honest with me, how she shows me all of her scars that she has received over the years, and how she doesn't judge me for my scars.

And I know that there is a part of her that loves me and wants nothing more than to have me love her in return. This is what scares me. I still have visions of my previous master. Those scars haven't healed.

I know what it is like to go unloved. Since I cannot be sure of my own heart right now, I don't want to be another guy that ends up hurting her. That would hurt me more than anything else I have endured so far.

Oct. 11, 2010

The wedding was amazing. I decided to do my hair up, which took me about an hour with Megan's help. She also helped me with the makeup. Thankfully we had enough time to get dressed and stuff before the wedding. I wanted to look perfect and not keep Jack waiting, especially since we made him get dressed two hours before we had to leave just so I could use the bedroom and then reveal the dress right before we left.

All of my efforts were worth it. I've never had a guy look at me the way that he did. I felt like a princess. He walked slowly over to me and whispered in my ear, "In case I forget to tell you tonight, you're the most beautiful girl at the wedding."

He then held his arm out for me to take. "Shall we?"

The wedding was about 20 miles outside of town, which gave us a little time to brief me again on everybody that was going to be at the wedding. He told me how to handle his mom, dad, grandparents, brother, sister, aunts, and uncles. We've been going over all of this for the past week. I just hoped that I wouldn't embarrass him too much in front of his family.

When we pulled into the church's parking lot, he got out, walked over to my side of the car, and opened the door for me. He then extended his hand for me to take and helped me get out. And he walked me to the front doors of the church with me clearly on his arm.

As we got inside, he started to slip his fingers in between mine. I found out that the guy coming over to us in a tux was his older brother, Max.

"What up, little bro? Mom was wondering who you were going to bring?"

With great civility, Jack introduced me. "Max, this is Liselle. Liselle, this is my older brother."

Max then shook my hand and told me how great it was to meet me before he tacked on a, "So are you and my brother...?"

I deferred to Jack on that one. Thankfully, he didn't waste any time to say, "We're together."

"Oh, Jack, man. You're going to have come up with something better than that. Mom and Nana are going to nail you on that. You've only been broken up with Brittany for a month."

I was happy for Jack to say that we were together, but Max brought up a good point. It had only been about a month since the break up with Brittany. It would look bad for me if Jack declared having strong feelings for me in that amount of time. And I didn't want to be introduced to his mother as the girl that he has been spending his nights with for the past month. Mothers judge you on that sort of thing.

I think Max could see me looking at Jack as he was waiting to come up with another term for us. "Dude, if you're going to introduce her as your girlfriend, Mom will be all over you two tonight. She won't stop until she finds out how you met and what the first date was like. And don't forget that Mom loved Brittany. She is still wondering what happened between you two."

And then I think Max thought of how this might sound in front of me be he added, "Frankly, I think you're a definite upgrade from Brittany. And in case he hasn't told you yet, he's totally in to you."

"Do you see what I mean about my brother having no shame", Jack said while blushing.

"I'm just trying to help you out. I can't help it that you're letting a beautiful girl like this carry on with you without giving her the proper title for your feelings for her."

Jack became speechless at this point. Thankfully I remembered what he had told me about his brother, so I said, "With what he's giving me, I'm not too concerned about the proper title."

I then took Jack's arm and walked into the sanctuary to take a seat. His brother just stared at us.

Jack thanked me for that and then asked me not to do that kind of stuff in front of his mom, grandma, or sister.

"You know, you're going to have to define what we are before I meet your mother."

"I know", was all he said.

"And if your brother can tell that you are totally in to me, the women in your family will be able to tell."

That's when Jack just looked at me. "How do you want me to define us?"

I don't know if it is something in us as women or whether it's something that we learn as we grow up, but it always seem like a bad idea to let a guy know that you like him or to tell him how you would like to define your relationship with him.

Maybe it has something to do with guys' innate ability to just copy what you say. If you say "I love you", the guy will just repeat it. It's not that this echo of your affection isn't sincere. It's just that you would like to hear it from him first.

"I want you to define us by how you feel about me."

I wouldn't find out his answer until later that night at dinner. We were sitting with his mom, dad, and sister. Jack called it the great inquisition where we were bombarded with questions about how we met, how long we have known each other, etc.

I didn't come off very good during this part, but Jack kept trying to make my answers sound better. But there was no way to explain the ring on my left ring finger, especially when Jack's mother said, "You know, I saw on *Dr. Phil* the other day about how people that come out of relationships that have lasted a long time start to sleep around to get a feeling of self-worth. People do a lot of stupid things when they are getting over a break up."

"Mom, the ring on Liselle's finger is from me. I bought it to give to Brittany when I was going to propose to her. But a funny thing happened when I got down on one knee. She told me that she had been sleeping with Steve."

Jack was more than a little defiant. And as he continued, he took my hand.

"I can't tell you what is going on between me and Liselle. It's not because I'm ashamed of it. I just can't define it. I just know that when I am with her that I feel things that I haven't felt in a long time when I was with Brittany.

And that ring is a promise to help to make me a better person. Despite what you might think of a person that you just met, Liselle is more worthy of that ring than Brittany ever was."

"I have no doubt that you find a certain worthiness in her, considering that you have been sleeping together ever since the breakup."

There was a look on his mother's face that I have seen plenty of times on a mother's face. I guess, fortunately enough for me, this time I was with Jack.

"I hate to tell you this, Mom, but two people of the opposite sex can share a bed and not have sex. Just ask any married man. Right, Dad?"

The entire table was shocked and speechless. Jack's mom and sister were especially. Jack's dad was just laughing. He didn't even stop when his wife hit him

Jack then turned to me. "Would you care to dance?" And we exited the entire situation and danced.

I apologized for causing him so many problems with his family. He said that it wasn't my fault and that his mom and sister really liked Brittany and thought that she was the one.

It felt good to be with him. I liked having his arms around me. I've never had a guy stand up for me before. I've had plenty of mothers hate me without ever having gotten to know me, so I was used to that. I ended up telling Jack this as we were dancing.

We talked a lot as we were dancing. We talked about very private stuff. And no matter how much we shared, there was always more. And we continued like this all night, even on the car ride home and once we got to bed.

Bedtime was nice. He only wore a pair of boxers. I started off wearing a tank top and a pair of panties. We just laid in bed, facing each other, with our arms around each other, and looking into each other's eyes as we continued to share the deepest parts of ourselves that we haven't shown to anybody in a very long time.

It's not that we were ashamed of our secrets. It was everything that we wanted to get off of our chests. We just couldn't find anybody that was worthy of keeping our secrets without judging us.

I do love him. I'm not going to kid myself, even if I won't tell him. And the more that I am with him, the more that I love him.

His mom did apologize to me. She said that she was glad that I was taking care of her boy during this difficult time. And his father cut in while I was dancing with Jack. I danced with his father as he apologized for Jack's mom and asked that I didn't think poorly on his family. I told him that I couldn't. I've thought better of the world since I've gotten to know Jack.

The Dance (II)

By

Jack Webber

There are moments in your life that you thought would only happen once, and then they happen again and seem to be just as special.

When I danced with Liselle this weekend, it was not the first time that we have danced together. There shouldn't have been anything extraordinary about it. I've known her longer than the time that I danced with Brittany for the first time. And yet in many ways, dancing with Liselle was by far superior to that first time with Brittany.

Comparing the two women and the two events, I can only hope to understand myself a little bit better.

In terms of clothing, the women seemed to be identical. Brittany wore a jade green dress. Liselle wore a dark blue dress. Both looked amazing in them. Brittany looked so good that I found the courage to ask her to dance when I didn't even know her.

I can't hold this against Liselle, since I have known her before the dance. I wanted to dance with Liselle because she looked so hurt by what my family was saying. I wanted to hold her close to me and take the pain away. She is too beautiful to be sad on my account.

Being a guy, I can say that in terms of dancing ability, both women are equal.

My first dance with Brittany had me extremely aroused. I was a horny teenage boy. I should give Brittany some points for agreeing to go out with me when the first thing she noticed about me were my raging hormones.

But Liselle gave me great conversation as we danced. And when I was dancing with her, I didn't want the dance to end. And bonus points should be given to Liselle for encouraging my hormones during the lighter moments of the dances.

So what made the dances so special and yet so different?

As much as I hate to admit it, my dance with Brittany was special because it was an illusion. I've been telling myself that it was something special for so long because it made for the telling of a great love story. It would be a story for our kids. But as I look at it, I was just a horny teenage boy, who saw an attractive girl, asked her out, and ended up dating her for four years.

And as I am learning, most of my relationship with Brittany seems to have turned out to be a lie and nothing more than a tale that I believed for so long.

But what made dancing with Liselle so wonderful was that she was dancing with me. It was the way that she looked at me and put her head on my shoulder. It was what she said to me and didn't say to me. It was what my parents said to her and the pain that I wanted to take away from her.

All of my life I have been trying to write the perfect love story. Over the years I have written out all of the girls before Brittany. Those romances were so short lived and junior high that I could do so without any real moral problems. But I stayed with Brittany for far too long to not consider her a part of my life.

Maybe I was trying to force a happy ending on a story that it didn't belong on.

But now I am stuck with a love story that comes out of the ashes of an illusion. How do you create a love story with a beginning like that? Do you tell your kids that you met their mother after some other woman rejected you? That's not very romantic.

My brother could tell that I was in love with Liselle. Maybe he knows me better than I know myself.

I know that I care a great deal about Liselle as a person. I have no idea what love is right now. I just know that the dance with her was special because it was with her and everything that she means to me.

A Mother Reason for Rehab

By

Jack Webber

Although Brittany and I started dating without any help from our parents, the fact that our mothers worked together didn't hurt our relationship. It meant that we got instant approval from the powers that be.

And it wasn't just that Brittany and I became a power couple within our families because of who we were. I had the extra responsibility of the fact that I was the middle child with an older brother that was not known for long relationships and a little sister that was known for lengthy relationships with guys that were a little on the unusual side.

Brittany and I were seen as a normal, well adjusted couple that could go the distance. In our relationship, my mother saw the real opportunity for one of her children to get married to a person that she would like for us to get married to. And it didn't hurt that she would have liked the possibility of Brittany's mom as an in-law.

I didn't notice it at the time, but there was a lot of pressure on us to be this couple. It wasn't as bad in the beginning as we were getting to know each other. After the one year mark and as we were starting to show that we could last as a couple during the college years, the pressure began to grow.

There were more family events where we were barraged with questions about when we were going to get married. It hung over us like a cloud. We laughed it off saying that we still in college and that it wasn't a good time to get married, but there was a feeling as if our marriage was just a matter of time. We were even being treated as a married couple.

I was invited to family events with Brittany's family. Our parents even worked out Thanksgiving and Christmas dinners, so that Brittany and I could make it to both sides of the family. We both went on family vacations with each other's family and received presents from what was supposed to be our future in-laws on our birthdays and Christmas.

I know that my mom wants me to get back together with Brittany. It doesn't matter to her that she cheated on me. That could be forgiven. My mom just wants me to go back to dating a type of girl that she would approve of.

I think this is unfair to Liselle. She is being compared to Brittany without even getting the chance to be herself. My brother and dad seem to like her. Guys are always more open to the idea of dating another person. Women are harder to please, especially your mother.

My mom will say that she wants what is best for me. Staying with somebody that cheated on me is not the best thing for me. And maybe that's not what she is trying to tell me. Maybe she just wants me to be careful as I learn to get over the heartache.

Spending so much time with Liselle probably isn't the smartest thing I've done. I thought that when we started this that we would just use each other to get over the previous relationship. Once healed, we would go our separate ways and be better off. The self-destructive behavior that typically befalls people in our situation wouldn't exist.

I'm finding, however, that I do care for Liselle. I'm just not sure how deep that caring is. I've tried to scale it back lately, since I am getting the feeling that Liselle is looking to me as a lover. I like her too much to try to go down that road with her when I'm in the shape that I'm in. I don't want to hurt her by my inability to love.

And I know that I shouldn't feel this way, but I feel like I disappointed my mother by breaking up with Brittany, like it is somehow my fault that Brittany cheated on me. It's not like I haven't thought about the breakup and wondered if I did something wrong that would have caused her to cheat on me.

Being a guy, I will never tell my mother that I feel like a disappointment. I also won't tell Liselle the full extent of the rehab that I need. Women can say what they want about guys not listening because we are too busy trying to fix the problem. Women are always too busy trying to fix men to ever hear our problems.

Oct. 15, 2010

Jack took me out for a hayride tonight. I don't know if this was a date or not. We had been going on dates, and then he decided that it would be better if we didn't date because it would only end up hurting me. Then he went down on me, invited me to a wedding, and stood up for me in front of his parents. So I'm not exactly sure what is going on in his head.

He is picking things to do with me that are romantic in tone. And he has been very affectionate in bed as well as elsewhere. It's been a long time since I have felt this way about a guy. Usually a guy will have his hands all over you because he gets off touching you. With Jack, you can tell that he's not touching me because the boobs just happen to be attached to me. He's touching me.

Maybe he was right to not date me anymore because he was afraid of hurting me. We were only sleeping together and being romantic because it was a way for us to keep from hurting somebody else. We were both hurting when we made this agreement. To think of our pain at a moment like that wasn't exactly possible.

The rehab part of the plan has worked wonderfully. When I first met him, I had been sleeping with guys on the first or second date. I would even sleep with guys that I brought home from the bar without them even taking me out first. I had forgotten what it felt like to have somebody actually care for me and want to be with me.

We still haven't had sex. I think he is afraid to. It's not because it will be his first time. I think he is afraid that if we have sex that it will be finally closing the door on the Brittany era of his life. She might have slept with somebody else, but he still carries a glimmer of hope that they will get back together.

I bought a box of condoms the other day and put them in a place where he would see them. He made a comment to me about them. I told him that I just wanted to be prepared in case things started to go in that direction some night. Then I laughingly added that if I didn't use them with him that I would use them with the next guy that came along.

He seemed kind of hurt by this, and I regretted it as soon as I said it. I tried to apologize. "I'm sorry. There's just times when I wonder how long we're going to last. I mean, we are just using each other. Neither one of us had said that we care about the other."

Jack kissed me on the forehead and held me closer to him. "I'm not a stray dog. You don't have to worry about my owner coming here someday and asking for me back."

And he was right. Our former lovers aren't going to want us back, but that doesn't mean that we aren't stray dogs with no owner and no place to go.

I love him. It would be easier for me to just have sex with him, at least then I wouldn't care about him and the possibility of losing him. But as it is, I am falling for him more and more each day. I know that he has had his heart broken, but I could love him more than she did.

Sometimes I think he knows this. There are times that I know that he cares for me. Then there are times that I know that he is thinking about her.

I've thought about telling him how I feel about him, but I think that usually ends up scaring a guy away more than helping a girl out. Guys see it as being too strong and sometimes creepy. I don't want him to think that I'm some crazy, psycho girl.

So I can go on loving him and hope that someday he will truly love me in return. I will have to put off these feelings that he won't be healed in time to love me. I will just be healing him for the next girl that is fortunate enough to date him.

Halloween is coming up in a few weeks. I will see what he decides to do for a costume. We're supposed to go to some parties. I'll see if he wants to do a couple's costume. That is usually a pretty good sign that a guy likes you.

After that we will have the holidays coming up. I would like to invite him to my parents' place for Thanksgiving, but I think this would be some of the psycho, creepy girl behavior.

And then will come Christmas, which will have to be celebrated a little bit before since the semester leaves before the actual holiday. I want his gift to be special. I've already been thinking of things to get him that would be appropriate for a friend to give him while still showing him that I care for him as something more than a friend.

I wish I were a guy. Then I could just tell him that I love him and give us some sort of official status. Women have to wait for the man to make up his mind. You never know whether to encourage the man and make him feel safe to tell you what you think he is feeling, or whether you should act like you don't care, so that he wants you even more. Either way, it hurts waiting.

Prince Eric in a Can

By

Jack Webber

The other night in bed, I was morbidly curious as to what first attracted her to Steve. Having known Steve for the majority of my life, I wanted to see how I compared to what she found attractive. The actual intelligence of this is questionable. The woman has said that she thinks I am good looking and have a sexy body. She seems to want me to love her.

The problem is that although women think they are being obvious, their clear signals oftentimes get confused. Was she touching her hair just then because she was trying to signal her interest in me, or was it in her face? Was that slight touch accidental or on purpose? And when they say that you are handsome, do they mean it, or are they saying it because they would want somebody to tell them that? If guys are supposed to tell a woman that the dress looks good on them, then what is the point of asking us if it makes them look fat? Are they wanting a lie? If we love them enough to spare their feelings with a lie, is that better than a truth?

And that is what confuses me about women. Sometimes something means one thing. Another time it means something entirely different. So when I asked her what attracted her to Steve, I didn't know how to take her answer.

At first, she avoided the question. Do I take that as she is completely over Steve? Or do I take that as she is not over Steve, and she doesn't want me to compare myself to him because I would lose in the comparison?

I let her not answer it the first few times, and I would let it drop for a few minutes before bringing it up again. After about an hour of slipping it into other conversations after having promised her that I would let it go, she finally answered it.

She said part of what attracted her to Steve was the fact that he had jet black hair and blue eyes. She said that she has always found this combination sexy. And then she started talking about *The Little Mermaid* and how that was her favorite of the princess movies. She wanted to save a prince, give up something of herself in order to get a chance to be with the guy, and then get the guy to realize that she was the one that saved him.

And all I got from that was that she liked Steve because of his black hair and blue eyes, which is what I told her. And then she got mad that that was all that I heard from her story. She then said that although Steve fit the bill of her prince in terms of looks that he wasn't really the prince that she had been looking for.

I then asked her if she thought I would look good with my hair darker. I already had blue eyes. My hair was a lighter shade of brown.

This question then made her mad. She said that she liked me the way that I was and that I shouldn't compare myself to Steve. She then said that women sometimes find one thing attractive with one guy and then something completely different to be attractive with another guy. There is a guy variance of sexy qualities.

I'm just trying to figure out what she likes so I can try to see if I meet her requirements. Instead she gives me a shifting scare of what she finds attractive. Does she really think I'm attractive, or is she just telling me that? Does she want me to change without telling me that she wants me to change? Or could she possibly really think that I am perfect the way that I am?

Oct. 17, 2010

With the hayride on Friday night and no mention of anything else for the weekend, I had put all hope for a Sweetest Day with Jack away as just some stupid girl fantasy.

He had gotten Megan to take me out shopping and do "girl" stuff as he called it. I hadn't really thought anything about it. Jack is good at giving me space and letting me hang out with my female friends.

And it felt good to discuss my problems with and feelings for Jack with Megan. I thought that maybe she could tell that I was having problems. It just turned into a nice girl's day out.

When we came back home, Jack was sitting in the living room. As soon as we entered, he stood up like he was presenting himself to somebody important. He was wearing a shirt and tie and had a bouquet of roses in his hand.

He looked really handsome and really nervous and unsure of himself. I wasn't much better. I was speechless. Thankfully Megan took my bags and pushed me towards him before going into her bedroom and shutting the door behind her.

In one of the more awkward moments of our relationship, we just looked at each other and didn't know what to say. I was just so happy that I didn't want to ruin it. And maybe I was waiting for him to finally tell me that he loves me. It's always best to just kind of let a man dangle out there by himself at such moments. It lets them stammer a little bit more so that they can spit out the right words that they have been trying to say.

Jack's words were, "Here I got these for you", as he handed me the bouquet of roses.

I thanked him and wished him a Happy Sweetest Day. He half-heartedly wished me a Happy Sweetest Day in return.

"Are you okay? You seem to be acting strange", I said as I was putting the flowers in water.

"No, I'm fine. I just..."

"Oh, God, Jack. I'm sorry. I didn't know we were celebrating Sweetest Day. I didn't get you anything. Although I don't know what you usually get a guy for these holidays. I usually just have sex..."

And that's when I stopped talking and didn't look at Jack.

He came up behind me and put his arms around me and said, "If it makes you feel any better, I forgot about Sweetest Day, too."

"But the flowers..."

"It's the one month anniversary of the first time we kissed."

For some reason, not remembering the first time we kissed when it was special enough for him to remember didn't make me feel any better. And maybe I should have remembered it. It was the first time in our relationship where we started to act like we were more than friends sharing a bed.

And I wished my mind would have spent more time on thinking about how I didn't remember the anniversary of the first time I kissed him. But there was this part of me that realized that if he was celebrating the first time we kissed as some sort of anniversary that he must really care about me.

And that's when I blurted out, "I love you!" He kind of jumped when I said it, which I can't blame him. It didn't sound very affectionate. With all of the excitement of the moment and thinking that he actually loved me, I just kind of yelled it... in a very scary way.

It was bad enough to say it, but to say it like that was just stupid. It came out like I was some crazy stalker girl, which I am probably a little bit obsessed with him. I'm just obsessed with him in a moderately normal and healthy way considering we've been sleeping together in a consensual way.

And I just waited for him to say something and to get me out of this situation. Of all of the things he could have said, he said, "We have reservations at 6. You should probably get dressed."

A simple "I love you, too" would have been nice. Even if he would have sounded scared and unsure of himself, it would have been better to at least hear that he loves me. I mean, who doesn't tell you that they love you right after you tell them that you love them?

Unless he thought that it was like the whole blowjob comment and that I didn't really mean it. I could see him doing that. I've given him plenty of opportunities to not take what I say seriously when it just comes out of nowhere.

Of course, he could have also thought that I was just saying it to cover up for the fact that I had forgotten it was the anniversary of the first time we kissed.

I discussed all of this with Megan as I was busy getting dressed. And it may have taken me a little bit longer to get dressed. We had to try to decide what dress would be best in a situation where a) I had forgotten that it was the one month anniversary of the first time I kissed a guy I'm in love with. b) I had just scared the guy that I'm in love with by shouting my feelings for him. And c) I had to make him know that I was romantically interested in him in a perfectly normal and acceptable way.

With everything that the dress had to convey, it took me a while. And it wouldn't have been so bad, but I also told Megan that I wanted the dress to say that I wanted to sleep with him tonight while not looking cheap or desperate.

That's when Megan snapped at me. "Jesus! You seriously can't keep a man without fucking him, can you?"

And then I started crying. But she was right. Over the years, I would cover up all of the stupid things I would say by just having sex with the guy. It's just that I learned that having sex distracted the man from all of the crazy stuff that I would say or do. It somehow made it be socially acceptable to be a nut job.

Like if Jack had been like any other guy I've dated, I would have just started kissing him while undressing him after I had yelled my affections for him. By the time the sex would have been over, he would have totally forgotten about what I had said. And everything would be normal between us, like it never happened at all.

So between the sobs and the inaudible crazy talk coming out of my mouth, Megan somehow figured out what I was saying. She hugged me and told me that I had a guy out there that loved me, even if he couldn't say the words. She also said that I need to take it slowly with him. He's learning to love again and is trying to make sure that he doesn't get hurt by love this time around.

Once I got dressed, Jack took me out to dinner. It was a really nice restaurant. Everything was perfect, but it was all wrong. There was just this tension between us where we weren't even acting like ourselves.

"I'm sorry that I screamed 'I love you' at you earlier. I just... And I'm sorry that I forgot it was the anniversary of the first time we kissed. You put a lot of thought into tonight."

"It wasn't that hard. All I had to do was think of you."

And that's when I said it. "I love you!" It wasn't as loud as last time. Still it was pretty scary sounding.

He just looked at me and said, "Are you okay tonight?"

I didn't want to tell him that I was madly in love with him. It's better to secretly love somebody and not to have that love returned than to declare your love and not have it returned. It might not seem like much of a difference, but at least a secret love allows you to continue to be around the object of the affection. A rejected lover tends to throw you out with your proposal.

So I told him that I was perfectly fine. He should just ignore me today since it was my time of the month.

I know I shouldn't blame something like this on my time of the month, but guys are all too willing to believe anything you say and do just by putting the blame for it on your period. They won't even question it, if you start acting normal again in a couple of days, which gave me a very small window of opportunity to get everything worked out emotionally with Jack. I mean, I'm sure that I could stop screaming that I love him in a horrifying way in the next couple of days.

Anyway, dinner went on in a mostly uneventful and awkward way. I think Jack wanted to talk, but the whole female problem kind of scared him away from talking about anything, especially if it had to do with feelings.

After dinner, Jack took me to the aquarium. He was kind of distant, which I thought was odd. Actually I thought the aquarium was odd for an anniversary type of thing to do.

"Thank you for taking me to the aquarium. I really like it." I tried to say it with the most sincerity that I could. I just really didn't know why he would take me here when he was so good at picking out date things to do.

"I'm glad you like it. I didn't know where else to take you for an anniversary celebration." He seemed as though he had put a lot of thought into it.

I didn't know why a bunch of fish would make him think of me, so I asked him in the most un-embarrassing way that I could.

And as he told me about how he chose it because I liked *The Little Mermaid* when I was little and always thought that it was romantic, I realized just how much effort he did put into making this date perfect.

And it wasn't just that he had thought of me. It was that he had been listening to me all of those times when I had just been rambling. He paid attention and actually remembered the stupid stuff that every other guy had ignored.

As this hit me, I stopped in the middle of the aquarium and was completely numb, while feeling a lot of different things at the same time. Jack just looked at me. He kind of was bracing himself for whatever horror was going to come screaming from my lips.

Not really knowing what I was doing, I walked slowly over to him and never lost eye contact with him. He started to look around to see how many people were going to be witnesses of what he was sure was going to be some psycho-crazed woman on her period.

That's when I kissed him. And more than just kissing the man that I loved, I was kissing the man that tried to fulfill my stupid little girl obsession with trying to find the perfect man in the form of a handsome prince.

And while he was still in shock and unsure of what had just happened, I whispered softly and sweetly in his ear that I loved him.

He looked at me like he was still confused about what was happening. So I stepped back a little to give him a little space and to show that I wasn't totally crazy.

"I've been trying to tell you that all night. It's just come out wrong every time."

And when he didn't say anything and looked like he was stuck in some sort of coma, I got scared and ran off crying. I didn't know where I was going to go. I just had to get away from him and from the perfect night that he tried to make for me and I ruined.

I'm not sure what happened next exactly. The next thing I know, I felt some resistance on my arm as I was running. And then I turned around to see what it was. Then I was kissing him.

When we stopped kissing long enough to take a breath, I was the one that was in shock. He seemed alert enough to notice the group of people just staring at us. "Do you want to finish looking at the aquarium, or would you like to go home?"

Not being entirely in my right mind, I said, "I'm going to fuck you."

He looked at me, nodded his head, and said, "Let's go home."

That was the longest car ride I have ever been on, even with Jack speeding and running a couple of the stop signs. When we got home, Megan was surprised to see us so early. I mouthed that we were going to do it and then told Jack to wait for me in the bedroom while I got freshened up.

When I got back into the bedroom, Jack was waiting for me. He was sitting there in a t-shirt and boxers. He still had his socks on. He looked really cute. I walked as sexily as I could and started to kiss him.

He pulled out of the kiss and said, "I really like you."

"I really like you, too, Jack."

But before I could start to kiss him again, he stood up. "That's just it, Liselle. I can't say that I love you. I don't think that we should do this until I can say that. It's not fair to you."

Oh, My God! I know that I've given guys blue balls before, but Jack is the first guy to ever give me a blue heart. I could understand him not wanting to sleep with me the first night that we spent together. But he likes me know. He even really likes me, which is totally code for "I'm on the verge of being in a relationship with you." Really liking me is a step beyond Facebook's "It's complicated."

And I don't know why, but I ended up saying, "What the hell, Jack. You take me out on some of the most perfect dates I have ever been on, and then you end up telling me that you only just really like me after I say that I love you."

"I just want to be sure that you don't get hurt", was all he could say.

"Bull shit! You love me. You're just afraid that you're the one that's going to get hurt. I'm not like Brittany. I'm not going to do anything to hurt you. I'm not going to just suddenly one day end this with you. This is the relationship I have been looking for all of my life."

"Okay. Answer me this. How do you know that I love you?"

"You remembered the first time that we kissed which by the way, according to today's date, you were not counting the time that we were drunk and you first came home with me. That was the first time that we kissed. If today is the one month anniversary of our first kiss, then you must be counting the kiss the night that you told me I was beautiful, or the kiss the night of the party when we kissed in the shower."

"What's wrong with celebrating the one month anniversary of the first time when we kissed when I told you you were beautiful? It's the first night that I started to have romantic feelings for you. I'm sorry if I wanted to celebrate it with you."

"But you celebrated it by taking me to the aquarium. I didn't know why you would do that, until you brought up *The Little Mermaid*. You were trying to be the prince I have been looking for. You know that you could be that guy. You want to be that guy."

"Yes! I want to be that guy, but then I'm with you and start to doubt everything that I'm feeling. What am I going to do if I screw this up? Where will I turn?"

And as I watched him, he turned into the scared, lost little puppy that I found at the bar the night that Brittany left him. "And what if we have sex, and I'm not as good as the other guys that you've been with. Will you still love me?"

I sat down beside him and just held him. "You might not realize it, but our first time is not going to be about the actual sex. It's going to be about the expression of something deeper. And all couples are a little awkward at sex the first few times. It's a matter of getting to know the other person, their technique, and getting into a rhythm with them. That's something that we will be learning together. And it has nothing to do with your lack of experience or my..."

And he put his finger to my lips to keep me from saying how experienced I am. And we kissed a kiss of understanding.

As we were in bed that night, we both apologized for various things. He said that he was sorry if he did anything to lead me on, but that everything he did was because he cared for me. He's just dealing with a fragment of a heart right now and needs to take it slowly.

And I apologized for being so crazy tonight. And then I apologized for lying about it being my time of the month. I just didn't want him to think that I was crazy.

I really do love him. I will just be glad when he is able to do more than just really like me. It is making being with him part heaven and part heartache. I never know whether I am getting closer to us getting together or whether I will get hurt by a guy that is perfect for me and that just happened to come into my life at the wrong time.

All of this is making his kisses all that much sweeter. I lay in bed most nights and cherish being in his arms. Thankfully he has never caught me watching him sleep. He seems so at peace when he is with me. And he looks like he belongs there with me.

Of Like and Love

By

Jack Webber

When I first started dating Brittany, I was infatuated with her. I couldn't spend enough time with her. Since we were in high school, the time we spent together was in a few hours after school and a couple more hours on the phone. The weekends were reserved for actual dates.

After three weeks of this high school relationship, I told her that I loved her. There was no doubt in my mind at that time what I felt for her was love.

Telling her that I loved her was probably one of the biggest gambles of my life. She had never given me any real indication that she liked me as anything more than a friend. We had kissed and held hands, but she seemed to be taking her time getting to know me.

As I think back on it, I was clearly leading the direction of the relationship at that time. We were good throughout high school. The more that we got to know each other, the more the relationship grew stronger. We would need that strength during the summer between high school and college as we were all that we had during an unpredictable change in our lives.

Our first year of college was also good. We were each other's support system. As we enjoyed more freedom, we grew closer together instead of farther apart.

The summer between our freshman and sophomore years was one of the best summers of our lives. Instead of depending on each other for a sense of security, we could actually enjoy each other's company.

We almost had sex that summer. Being a guy, I thought that we should have already had sex. We had discussed it several times throughout our relationship. She would always tell me that she loved me, but that she wanted to wait until marriage.

That summer was our golden era. It was carefree and fun. We were no longer two stupid kids in high school. We loved deeper and were more like an adult couple.

When we returned to school in the fall, our relationship was the strongest it had ever been. Maybe I had gotten too secure in that feeling. Maybe I started to take the relationship for granted and stopped working on it.

Our work schedules and class schedules changed. We did spend less time together, but the time we did spend together was good and free of conflict.

Looking back on it now, I can see that we were fueling the relationship on the past. We had fallen into a rut and kept on following the same patterns that had worked for us in the past.

During this time, we told each other that we loved each other countless times, but each time it was becoming more and more a lie. By this past summer, we were no longer a couple in love. We had just grown used to each other and were afraid to admit that something that was once so perfect had started to go wrong.

I've asked myself a million times since the breakup why I asked her to marry me. I think I knew the relationship was having problems. The thought of not having her in my life scared me more than an imperfect relationship.

Instead of being in love with Brittany, I really liked her. I cared about her as a person and didn't want to see her get hurt. We should have broken up some time last year, but we allowed our relationship to endure.

Looking back on it now, I realize that I asked her to marry me because it was the next step and my last chance of keeping the relationship together.

There are times that I wish you could have funerals for people, places, things, and events in your life that are over. Brittany and I should have pulled the plug on our relationship at least a year before it actually ended. We could have held a little service for each other, mourned the loss of what once was, and then moved on.

The denial on both of our parts is what hurts the most. We just chose to deal with it in different ways. She chose to look for love somewhere else.

I chose to continue the lie that was our relationship.

I don't know what is happening between me and Liselle. She says that she loves me. I only know that I feel about her like I did with Brittany as the sun was starting to set on our relationship. Only I feel a little bit more for Liselle.

Liselle confuses me and comforts me. If I'm falling in love with her, it's nothing like when I fell in love with Brittany. Maybe that's not being fair to Liselle. Maybe love doesn't come the same way every time. Maybe that's why we keep looking for it and sometimes miss it when it is right there in front of us.

I just don't want to get hurt again. Liselle is all I have right now. If I lose her, I will never be able to recover.

All's Fair
By
Jack Webber

I have always been told that all is fair in love and war. I can somewhat agree with the war part. If you have the ability to totally annihilate your enemy, go for it. People's lives are at risk. It's better to destroy another people that will always be nameless and faceless to you than to have a bunch of your own people die and to have wounded soldiers walking around your town.

War is a nasty business that is all about winning. To make it beautiful and sanitary is beyond reason. What is fair is not really a question one should be asking when it comes to war. Why should one innocent civilian die while another lives? Why does one soldier live while the one standing next to him dies?

It matters to the loved ones at home. We would like for death to be fair. We can blame God and tell him that we think it's not fair. As much as it hurts, death is fair. We all have to go through it at some point. Nobody can ever escape it. So whether we do it early in life or later is just a matter of timing.

But if I can say something about death, it is that it is the great equalizer. The rich and the poor are the same when they're six feet under.

But love… Ah, now that is something entirely different. If God is love and we want a fair and just God, then love should be fair.

Love isn't like war. It's not about winning. It's about another human being. If you want to possess somebody's affection so badly that you are willing to cheat to call that person yours, then you will never really have that person. You can have that person physically, but the heart can only be given by the person to whom it belongs.

I guess, in a way, that love isn't fair. You can love somebody and never have them love you in return. But love is fair in that each of us are given a heart to love with, and we can love whomever we want with that heart, even if the love isn't reciprocated.

This is the problem that I am facing now. Somebody has declared their love for me. I really like them. They are very special to me, and I would be lost without them. And I am physically attracted to them. I just can't honestly tell them that I love them.

I've told them this because it is the right thing to do to be fair to them. I've been hurt by love before. I could have used this other person and claimed that it was all fair in love and war, but that is thinking about love as war.

When you take the time to actually discuss your feelings with another party and stop thinking solely about your wants and desires, you find that love conquers war.

Oct. 21, 2010

Ever since I told Jack that I loved him, he has been less passionate with me. He still holds me affectionately, looks at me longingly, and listens to everything I say.

Maybe the problem didn't start exactly right after I said that I loved him. It has gotten worse since then. Thinking back on it, it really started a little after I squirted on him, but he seemed okay with it right after it happened. At least, he was there for me.

I know that he keeps saying that he is trying to not hurt me, but he's hurting me more by making me think that he really does love me and won't admit it. I've had my heart broken a million times. I prefer that to getting signals from a guy that only fan the flames of hope that he could ever love me

Lately when I am in the comfort of his arms, I have been going over every conversation we have ever had. Since we started out just using each other, I might have been a little bit too open with the amount of guys that I've been with.

I got myself tested today for STDs at the health center. I don't know why I did it, except that it's a good thing to do every now and then.

Ever since I met his mom, I have felt a little bad about myself. I haven't met a lot of my boyfriends' moms. Maybe I'm not the kind of girl that you bring home to Mom. Jack thought I was, though. He even defended me in front of his. That has to count for something when it comes to whatever he is truly feeling and is afraid to show.

And maybe he is holding off on being more intimate because he has seen what the previous guys have done to me. Maybe he doesn't want to be one of those guys and wants to wait until he can be sure that he is able to love me.

Either way, I shouldn't really complain. He has been a better man to me as a friend than most of the guys that I've dated. Besides how I feel about him, I like how I feel when I am with him. I just hope that I can keep him and make him feel like I do.

Oct. 24, 2010

I got the test results back today. I don't have any STDs. I was really happy to hear it, and I wanted to tell Jack, except that I didn't quite know how. There's no good way to tell the man you love, "Hey, I know I was a bit of a slut before I met you, but I just got tested. You can screw me and not have to worry about catching anything."

There were so many times today that I wanted to tell him. I just felt ashamed. It's not that it's the first time I've been tested. I once dated a guy, Judson Roberts. I thought that I really loved him at the time.

He was really smart and really good looking. He had a beautiful smile and dimples. And he had the most beautiful blue eyes that were made even more beautiful by the fact that they were brought out by his perfectly tanned skin and dark black hair.

We had been going out for about a month and were about to get serious. And then we just suddenly stopped. He told me that he only fucked women that were disease free and that I should get tested because... "I know you've been around."

So I got tested. I felt so bad about myself and everything that I've ever done that I felt like I had to. I mean, Judson was so smart and handsome. If he rejected me, the man that would accept me would hardly be worth having. I figured that it was better to have him than to settle for the alternatives.

Once the results came in okay, we did have sex. Well, we didn't have sex immediately. I had to get on the pill. That's actually when I started to take the pill. Judson didn't like to wear condoms, so he made his girlfriends get tested before he would sleep with them. Sorry. "Fuck" them. I should use his words.

I think his objection to condoms was partly comfort. He said, "You wouldn't stick a bag over your head. Why would you stick one over your little buddy?" And he said something about pulling the hairs when he took it off.

He also gave me the environmental argument. He said that condoms were made of latex, which were made of oil. In addition to using up a non-renewable energy source, we would be filling up the landfills with bodily fluids and something that isn't biodegradable.

It sounded like a reasonable argument at the time, although I did question it a little. It was just that I thought that he was so smart that I didn't really want to appear to be even more stupid than I really am.

I thought a lot about Judson the other night as I was laying in bed with Jack with the knowledge of the test results, but, for some reason, I felt really ashamed about bringing up my test results to Jack.

When I finally got up enough nerve to tell him, he seemed really confused by my telling him that I had gotten tested. I tried to explain it as I was on the pill and that some guys don't like condoms for environmental reasons, or because they pull your dick hairs.

And Jack just looked at me as if I were crazy. He then kissed me on the forehead and said, "I've been living with you for over a month now. I'm not really worried about getting diseases from you. And in case you haven't noticed, I throw away the plastic bags that we get from the store instead of recycling them."

He then just laid down and tried to go to sleep.

That's when I told him about Judson.

Instead of judging me, he just said, "Liselle, I don't care about a woman's past before she knew me. I only care how she is when she is with me."

And as we talked, he said that neither I nor anything I did in the past was preventing him from making love to me. He said that he was going through a lot of stuff right now and that it was him who was the problem.

He seemed sincere. He has never lied to me and has always been honest with me. But I have had lots of guys say that "it's not you, it's me." And they always say this right before they're about to leave you.

I want to believe Jack and think that he's not like other guys. I just look at myself in the mirror and see what I look like naked. I know that I'm not the most intelligent girl, and that Jack probably would be better suited to somebody smarter. And I look at my past, and I see very little that would make him want me. There's a reason that guys sleep with me and never really have lasting relationships with me.

And then I look at Jack. I look at all of the wonderful things about him and how he could make any girl happy. I mean, he was willing to put off having sex with the girl that he really loved just because he respected her and her belief system.

I know when it's me and not the guy. I've fallen for enough men that have never been able to love me back to know what the problem is.

<u>The Lover's Cross</u>

By

Jack Webber

She tells her stories from her heart. And while she is focused on the narrative, her true meaning remains unspoken, but it is always present.

Tonight her story was about Judson Roberts. Her narrative was about how he had her get tested for STDs because he didn't want to use condoms. What remained unspoken was that Judson found it easier to control women by making them feel disease ridden. With their self-worth gone, obeying him and his every demand came easier. Who else would love them, except him?

But there was more that remained unsaid. She got herself tested the other day for my sake. She believed that I wasn't sleeping with her because of her past. As hard as I try, I can't get her to understand that there is nothing wrong with her as a lover.

If anything, I have discovered that she is the Jesus for the sins of my dating world. She feels hopelessly compelled to take on everybody else's sins as if they were her own. And for her pain, she has been rejected, ridiculed, and reviled.

As I hold her in my arms, I see a beautiful, young woman sacrificing herself on a cross, taking on my sins and pain, and only asking me to love her in return. I want to love her. It's just that I have been in love before. A part of me is still in love with somebody else.

The sad part is that I could truthfully tell her that I love her. I just can't get her to understand that I am not worth loving and that she doesn't need to suffer for my sins.

The longer I go without telling her how I feel about her, the more she drifts away from me. I will wake up one morning, and she will no longer be on the cross bearing my pain. And I will be alone looking for a savior that has gone.

Oct. 25, 2010

When I entered the bedroom tonight, Jack was waiting for me on the bed. He was dressed in only a pair of black boxer-briefs. He had set up several of small scented candles around the room. He didn't say anything. He just looked adoringly at me and motioned for me to take my usual place on the bed.

I sat down next to him, and we kissed for a minute. As we were kissing, he slowly undid my robe and slid it off of my shoulders. As he continued to kiss me, he gently lifted my tank top over my head. Since he kind of messed up my hair as he did it, he took his hand and straightened it up for me. It was really sweet.

At that point, I didn't really care if my hair was messed up or not. I planned on getting my hair really messed up, so I leaned in closer to him and told him that it was fine as I started to nibble on his ear.

As we kissed some more, he tried to undo my bra, but he was having problems. I really wanted him to do it. There's just something really hot about guy taking it off. I think it's that it shows that the guy knows his way around something that terrifies him. You can tell a lot about a guy by the way that he handles the entire bra issue.

I've had some guys who would never even try to unhook it. They would just take the straps off of your shoulder and then pull the cups down to reveal the sisters. They attacked the bra without any thought about how much it may have cost you. Guys like this usually attack your breasts just as aggressively as they handled the bra.

And then you have other guys that are so afraid of the bra that they will spend all of their time feeling the outside of it, or slipping their hands up underneath it. They want your breasts, but they don't want to show that they don't know how to take it off.

And you have some guys that won't even touch the bra. I once dated a guy that would have sex with me with my bra on. I got to the point where I would just take it off myself during sex.

And then there's Jack. When he started to have problems, he started to kiss me on the shoulders so that he could see how to unhook it a little better. But even when he was struggling with it, he still took the time to put the strap back up on my shoulder when it fell down.

After he had fiddled with it for a minute, including accidentally snapping it one time, which he did apologize for, he looked at me with a defeated look on his face. I waited for him to say that this was all just a mistake. Instead he said, "Can you help me with this?"

I've never had a guy ask me for help before. Most of them have been too macho. They have never asked for help with anything. Even when other guys have struggled with the whole bra thing, they just gave up. I took it off for them, and then they went to town as if I had just opened the doors to heaven. They couldn't get in there fast enough.

It was nice to have a guy admit that he needed help. It was even nicer in that Jack didn't act like Cookie Monster attacking a plate of cookies. Jack treated them like they were objects of beauty that should be touched delicately. He handled them with such care and attention that I found myself saying, "I've never liked my breasts. I've always thought they were too small."

He then stopped and looked at me. I didn't mean to make him stop. I guess he thought I wasn't enjoying it. He handed me my bra and said, "I can turn around while you get dressed, if you want."

There are times like this when he looks sad, scared, and shows just how he has been treated before by Brittany. Even if he didn't do anything wrong, he still feels responsible for it. There is something sweet about it. It's times like these when Jack breaks my heart. I think of all of the love that I could have given him over the years, if we would have just known each other.

"I don't want you to stop. I just... I've never liked my breasts. Most guys handle them like sex objects. You treat them like they're beautiful... like I'm beautiful."

Jack looked at me. I could tell that he was thinking about something, but that he was also struggling with his feelings. He then stood up decisively and said, "Take off your clothes."

I looked at him like he was crazy. He waited a minute for me to make a move. Then he just shook his head and took off his boxer-briefs.

"You're the first girl I've ever been naked in front of. How does my body compare to the other guys you've dated?"

And then I told him how hot he was. His abs are sexy, and he has that V-cut thing going on that actually goes down all of the way to his dick, which he is rather well-endowed.

"You didn't answer my question. How do I compare to the other guys you've dated?"

"I don't know. When I'm with you, I don't think about the other guys I've been with."

"Why did you bring up your breasts? What have other guys done when they were presented with them?"

As I stopped and thought about it, I thought about all of the guys that I have been with. And I don't know if he could read my face at that moment or not, but he came over to me and took my face in his hands.

"It's okay if you think of other guys. There have been times when I am with you that I have thought about Brittany."

"But you're still getting over her."

"Because you've been patient with me. How many guys have you gone out with trying to forget one person?"

And he was right.

"So when said I was seeing too much in you, you meant..."

"I meant that I really like you. You're just wanting something more serious than I can give you right now."

"Did you know that before you were about to sleep with me tonight?"

And it was the way that he laughed that made him so cute right now. "No. I've felt you slipping away lately. I thought that if I didn't sleep with you that I would lose you."

"Well, as somebody who has slept with guys to keep them from leaving, I have to tell you that it never really works out."

There was a silence from my embarrassment and his not knowing what to say next. That's when I looked down and without thinking said, "You're starting to..."

From the earlier arousal, he was starting to leak lubricant. Being me, I stopped it with my hand. Then there was the awkward moment where he's naked with his semi-flaccid penis leaking lubricant and I have my hand on the tip of his penis trying to keep it from getting onto the floor or the bed. It's always moments like that where you find yourself without a towel or Kleenex to clean it up.

As he apologized, became red with embarrassment, and confused as to what to do at that moment, I felt that it was appropriate to just rub the lubricant onto his dick. When I was finished rubbing it in, I smiled sheepishly and said, "There. That seemed so stop it."

He smiled back politely and said that he had better put his pants back on. He was really cute as he turned away from me to hide his penis that had just been exposed to me quite an amount of time. He has a really nice ass. He actually has an ass. Some guys are just a solid block of muscle or have really flabby asses. Jack's is toned. And he has those dimple things right where the back meets the ass.

Anyway, when he had his pants back on, we looked at each other. Neither one of us wanted to say the words that we knew one us was going to have to speak.

And with the kindness and graciousness that I have come to love about him, he smiled and said, "I could really use a friend right now. Do you mind if I spend the night?"

"Not at all. I will always be here for you."

I held out my arms for him. He walked over to me, and we hugged. It felt good to have my bare breasts pressed up next to him, even if we were breaking up at that moment. Still I felt slightly ashamed.

"I should probably put my bra back on."

"Please don't. Since this is our last night together, I would like to remember you the way that you are."

We spent the entire night in each other's arms. We were just facing each other, looking in each other's eyes, and saying everything that we had wanted to say for the past few weeks.

We laughed. Sometimes we cried. But in those hours we were everything that I loved about being with him.

In the morning, I helped him to pack up his few belongings. We loaded them in his car. And before he left, I gave him back his ring.

"Thank you for showing me what I've been missing."

He took the ring, put it in his pocket, and hugged me. "Maybe I can give it to you for real some day."

"I would like that."

As he smiled at me delaying his departure, I said, "You had better go now. I don't want you to see how I'm going to cry over you."

He accepted this and got in his car and drove off. I watched him go, not because I wanted to see if he would turn around and look at me, which he did, but because I couldn't move from that spot.

Megan eventually helped me inside. Neither one of went to classes. We spent the day talking. By noon I had gone through an entire box of Kleenexes. Even after all of the crying, I don't think she understood why Jack and I broke up. There was no fight. We both liked each other. He wasn't going back to Brittany. We didn't even really discuss breaking up last night. We just knew each other well enough that we could call it.

When a guy like Jack is willing to give me his virginity because he is afraid of losing me, I knew it was time to end it. We had promised each other that we would use each other to get over the previous breakup. I don't know if I helped him or not. If anything, he was starting to turn into me. At least we realized it and ended it before I could have destroyed him. He's far too beautiful a person to end up like me.

Despite the fact that I loved him, he made me realize that I still need to work on myself. That's something I haven't done in a very long time.

He has spent the past couple of weeks trying to keep me from getting more involved than I should. He was trying to keep me from getting hurt, knowing that he was still healing. But I kept pressuring him and fueling my school girl fantasies with the way things could be.

I didn't spend today crying over Jack. I spent today finally crying over all of the boys that I never let myself cry over before.

Home
By
Jack Webber

Today I finally went home to my own apartment. Steve was surprised to see me. We hadn't spoken since all of this mess started. When I entered, he just looked at me. And for the first time in almost two months, I saw my best friend standing there.

"Hey", was all he could say, and it was all I could say in response. As I walked closer towards him, I could see him start to tense up. He wasn't sure if I was going to punch him or not. I wasn't even exactly sure.

"Liselle and I decided to end it today." My pain at that moment was greater than my anger ever had been. With a shortage of sympathetic ears in my life, I couldn't help but to reach out to the one man I knew that would understand the woman I loved.

He offered me his apologies for everything that had happened. And like two old friends, we talked about our problems.

I have known Steve since kindergarten. At one point, he was my best friend. Somehow within the past two months, I no longer knew him.

He was sympathetic about Liselle. He shared some insight into her and her relationship with him. And it helped some, but I got the feeling that he didn't ever really get to know her the way that I did.

Out of politeness more than a morbid curiosity, I asked him how Brittany was. He told me about their relationship, how needy she is, and all of her faults.

Steve didn't tell me this, but he will be dumping her soon. The sex is no longer worth putting up with all of her drama.

I've only been gone from my old life for two months. Nothing really changed. I didn't think I changed either. How could one woman that I wasn't even dating change me without my knowing about it?

The only thing I am sure of is that home is a mailing address filled with the ghosts of people that I used to know. Something doesn't belong, and I fear that it is me. And as afraid as I am about this fact, I have nowhere else to go.

Welcome home.

Oct. 26, 2010

Jack called me last night. I was glad that he did. He said that he missed me. I told him that was part of the whole breaking up thing. He then reminded me that we weren't ever really dating, so we didn't have to follow the rules about breaking up.

I guess he has forgiven Steve. He said that he couldn't really be angry at a guy that introduced me to him.

I asked him if he had seen Brittany yet. I probably shouldn't have. With him calling me and acting like he didn't really want to end what we had, I wanted to know if he had seen her or felt anything for her.

He said that he hadn't seen her and that he wasn't going to go to the bars to look for a random hookup, either. I told him I understood and that I had given up on men for a little bit. My vibrator would have to satisfy me.

He asked me if I had my vibrator nearby. He then started to tell me that he was kissing me. The next thing I knew we were having phone sex. The sad part is that he was better over the phone than a lot of the guys I've done in person.

He even continued to talk after the sex. We spent the rest of the night on the phone talking about stupid stuff. It was so stupid that I can't even remember what it was about.

By two in the morning, we were both getting tired, but neither one of wanted to hang up. That's when Jack suggested that we put our phones on speaker. "Put yours on the pillow where I used to sleep, and we'll talk like we used to do."

"I'll put it on your side of the bed. I'm kind of hugging your pillow, while it still smells like you."

"You'll have to give me something to remember you by. All I have are the memories, and they aren't quite enough to comfort me tonight."

I don't know what time I fell asleep. I passed out talking to him and holding the pillow that he had been sleeping on since he started spending the night with me. When I woke up around 7 in the morning, I called his name. He didn't answer, but I could hear him breathing. That was enough for me.

I spent the next two hours waiting to see what he would do when he woke up. Hearing him say my name was worth it.

With our batteries about to die, we said goodbye and tried to go on with our day.

Oct. 27, 2010

After several texts and Facebook chats, I decided that I should probably give Jack something to remind him of me as he slept tonight, so I went over to his place and offered myself to him for his nightly comfort.

I didn't think about Steve answering the door. I had forgotten how little he talked. Of course, to be fair, I was dressed in a slightly inappropriate night gown to be knocking on somebody's door at nine o'clock at night. When I ignored his silence, I let myself in and was soon greeted with Brittany.

As soon as I saw her, I was looking around for Jack. It's always best to not get into a cat fight when you don't have a guy around to defend you. And Brittany had her claws out. Before I even got to the living room, she said, "My, we're looking slutty, Liselle. I thought you and Jack had broken up?"

"We have, but that doesn't mean she can't do an overnight visit, Brittany." And there was Jack with his calm, cool wit to defend me. "But I wouldn't expect you to understand that. You thought we were still in a serious relationship while you were fucking my best friend."

As he walked past Brittany, he couldn't take his eyes off of me. It had only been a day since we had seen each other, but it felt even better than I remembered to have his arms around my waist as he pulled me close to him and kissed me.

As he told me how beautiful I looked, Brittany stood beside Steve and glared at us. "Get a room. I feel like I'm going to catch an STD just watching you two."

"Well, considering I was screwing your boyfriend when you decided to screw him, you might want to get yourself checked out. Cause, I mean, I have slept with a lot of guys, so I passed on everything I had to Steve. And when you consider that I wasn't his first, you're probably pretty disease ridden there, Brittany. Your children are probably going to be born blind or something", I said as I walked by her.

And that's when Jack led me to his bedroom only stopping once to turn to Steve and Brittany to say, "Now if you will excuse us, we're going to be satisfying our carnal lusts."

Once we were in the safety of his bedroom, I turned to him and said, "What did you ever see in her?"

"I'm sorry. That was before I knew that there were women out there like you that flaunted their promiscuity while trying to turn me on."

And instead of judging me, he held me closer. I may not have felt it at the moment, but he told me again that I was beautiful. And I could tell by the way he held me and looked at me that he truly meant it.

"I'm sorry that I slept with all of the guys that I slept with before I met you."

But before I could say more, he stopped me and said, "You will never have to apologize to me for your past. It's not what caused us to break up."

"And what did cause us to break up?"

"Among many things, the fact that we were never really together. With all of the pretending, we couldn't tell what was imaginary and what was real anymore."

"I hate to tell you this, but that's common when you're in love."

"I know. I'm just hoping that this time I can have something I know to be real. I've spent too much time pretending because I was afraid of the reality that I was masking."

And he was right. I've spent too much time pretending to be in love with guys that I was no longer in love with or even physically attracted to even more. And I don't know at what point he knew that it wasn't working out between him and Brittany, but this was the first time he admitted that he continued the masquerade of their relationship instead of pulling the plug on what was an unresponsive relationship. Even when you know the relationship is on life support, you still hope that it can be fixed. It's painful to watch something die, even if you know it is time for it to end.

I don't know why I did it, but as I was with him, I asked him, "Do you still love her?"

"There are times that I miss her, but I don't know if that is same thing as love. I miss being able to spend time with her and Steve and to just have things the way it was for so long. But then I feel like it's trying to hold onto a life that no longer wants me, and that I have to let go of the past."

"Do you feel that way about me?"

"No. Saying goodbye to you the other day was the hardest thing I have ever had to do. At least when I broke up with Brittany, I didn't have to hide the fact that I loved her and was hurting at that moment."

"I hate to tell you this, but you've been doing a terrible job of hiding your feelings for me."

"I know, but you'll find that as you grow older, it's a lot easier to lie to yourself than to search your soul and admit to somebody else what you find down there."

I don't know why, but I kissed him. It wasn't a make out session. It wasn't passionate. And it wasn't leading anywhere. I was kissing him – his heart, soul, and entire being. And if he fought it in the beginning, he was soon kissing me back with his heart and soul.

I don't know how long we stayed that way. We seemed to be frozen in time. We were brought back to reality by the sound of Steve and Brittany having sex next door.

Jack looked at me and then I recognized the look on his face. It was the same as the other day when I told him that giving himself to me in an attempt to make me stay would only make him regret it. I didn't realize how I had crushed his spirit that day until that moment.

"When we have sex, I don't want you question your feelings for me. I've slept with guys that I shouldn't have because I thought that it would make them love me more, or make them stay once I started to feel them slip away."

As much as it hurt to admit this, I continued, "I can never take back all of the things that I've done, but I can finally know what it is like to love somebody and have them truly love me in return for the first time with you."

Instead of saying anything or kissing me, he just held me. And I was fine with that.

Teacher
By
Jack Webber

There is a certain danger in confronting a former lover in the early morning hours. Despite what you might be feeling at that moment, the past plays tricks on your senses. The smell of her perfume reminds you of happier times when you were more certain about your future.

Trouble sleeping?

Lying to her won't help. She knows you too well, so you just ignore her and hope that it's your mind playing a cruel trick on your heart. Your mind is the only thing that you can trust right now.

You know the breakup process works better if you don't let the woman you're trying to get over come over for a booty call.

Responding now would only encourage her. She acts as if she has a power over you. You're afraid to admit that she does.

Unless you aren't trying to get over...
What's her name?

Liselle?

Unless you aren't trying to get over Liselle. Even your mother could see what she really is. And I think that if you would admit it to yourself that you never really loved her. You were using her in a pathetic attempt to get over that one true love of your life.

As she lets her words sink in, she draws in closer to you to let the smell of her hair to tempt you, her eyes to tease you, and her mouth to taunt you.

As you turn to face her, a glimmer of victory shows in her eyes. You find yourself playing with her hair like you used to do. With each touch, she only encourages you more to give into her and her words.

I remember the first time that I saw you. You were a vision of loveliness, like an angel that had descended from heaven, a gift from God to make our lives better.

You taught me how to love and how truly great it could be to have a woman in my life.

As you start to caress her face and trace the outline of her lips with your fingers, she moans ever so slightly in agreement and starts to suck on your fingers.

> But of all the things that you've taught me, the one thing I remember the most is the lesson that you never meant to teach me.

You meet the horror in her eyes without flinching and continue.

> Steve has been my friend for as long as I can remember. I have been with him as we were discovering girls. I've seen the look in his eyes before. He's getting ready to dump you.
>
> You don't love me. You're just trying to beat him to the punch. I've learned your tricks.

She holds on to you desperately as you start to leave. She confesses her sins against you and professes her love.

You have dreamed of this moment from the time that she rejected you. All of the power that she took from you comes rushing back. And as you are about to deliver the justice that you longed for, all of the feelings of love and compassion temper your hatred.

And as she waits for your verdict, you aren't even sure of what will come out of your mouth. Do you stick the final knife in the past that you lost and twist it to make sure that it will never come back, or do you try to make peace with it?

There was a time when I would have given anything just to have you back again. From the time I was seventeen, I always thought you would be the one to complete my education. Instead you taught me when it's the right time to end a relationship.

So, Teacher, it's here that I must leave you.

But seeing that I have now surpassed you in knowledge, I will give you this advice. In the beginning, your self-worth will be at an all time low. You will think that nobody could ever love you.

Guys can smell that on a woman. You might think that by sleeping with them that they will like you. They will just be using you for sex.

When that happens to you, I hope you will remember what you have thought

> about Liselle. Then I hope you will think of me and realize that I saw more. Maybe someday another guy will see what I once saw in you.

And you leave her there. You know that there will still be days when you will think of her, but you will think of her differently.

Oct. 28, 2010

Jack was gone this morning when I woke up. He had left me a note saying that he didn't want to wake me, but that he had some things to take care of. He would see me later that night. At one point, he had written "I love you" in the note, but he had crossed it out.

I waited around his apartment for him. While I was watching the TV in the living room, Brittany came out and sat down next to me. I was going to ignore her, but she started talking to me as if we were old friends.

"Did Jack already leave? He's good at that, you know. He will say that he's busy working on some piece or whatever, but you never know with him."

I just looked at her.

"Of course, you really don't know about that, do you? You haven't been with him long enough to have him write anything for you, have you? You haven't even been with him long enough to get him to commit to you, have you?"

"Do you mind? I'm trying to watch this."

"That's fine. I just thought you would like to know that while you were sleeping last night, Jack snuck out of his room and met me out here on this sofa."

I tried to ignore her, but she continued, "I have to admit his technique has improved since meeting you. I should thank you for that, I guess."

I couldn't speak, and she took this opportunity to continue, "I'm sorry. Didn't he tell you? Steve and I are breaking up. Once it becomes 'official', Jack and I will pick up our previous relationship right where we left off."

I don't know why, but I started to punch the shit out of her. I was going for her face. Somehow I ended up on top of her, and she wasn't putting up much of a fight. I managed to dig all of my fingernails into her face and drag them across her face, before Steve came into the room and pulled me off of her.

Brittany started to get up at that point and would have fought me, except that Steve was keeping us apart as he was trying to get answers.

I had found my voice by that point and started screaming, "She's breaking up with you and is getting back together with Jack!"

And that kind of ended the fight. The fight was now between Brittany and Steve. I just wanted out of there. I wanted to be alone.

I don't remember driving home. I remember walking in the front door and Megan looking at me. I had been crying, but I totally broke down at that point. She held me as I told her everything that happened.

About three in the afternoon, Jack came barging into my apartment. He tried talking to me, but I yelled at him to go away.

And he did. He just left. He didn't even try to explain.

I guess we are truly over. He now has his precious Brittany back. He will no longer feel torn between which girl to love. His mom should be happy. I'm just a distant memory that will soon be forgotten.

Present Past Perfect Future
By
Jack Webber

There are a few times in life when your past rears its ugly head in your life and threatens your future. Last night I confronted Brittany and told her that I no longer loved her. It seems that this morning, she was no so willing to let me go now that her relationship with Steve is ending.

I don't know if she was honestly trying to get me back, or if she was trying to destroy what I had with Liselle. Either way, she decided to get rid of the Liselle problem by making her think I was getting back with Brittany. Liselle answered this declaration of war by scratching her face off.

I've seen her face. It's not pretty. Brittany tried to apologize to me. I guess once the Brittany-Liselle battle happened, the Brittany-Steve relationship battle finally happened. That didn't turn out so great for Brittany either. Steve dumped her.

Of all of the women that Steve has dumped, his dumping of Brittany was probably the most cruel. He took a picture of her messed up face after she had been crying over him and posted it on Facebook. He then changed his status to say, "I don't know who's the bigger bitch: Karma or my ex."

I don't know if it is Karma or not, but it hasn't been Brittany's day. And maybe I didn't help her any. After we had talked everything out, the way we probably should have before we actually broke up, I came back from the bathroom and found her naked in the living room.

I'm not sure what naked women in your living room usually say, but Brittany started with, "I'm sorry, Jack, and I want to make it up to you."

And I don't know what you usually do with a naked woman in your living room, but I found myself caressing her like I used to do.

As she started to kiss me, I started to fondle her breasts. The next thing I knew, I had guided her down to the sofa. She looked at me longingly, in a way that I had never seen her look at me before, as she slowly spread her legs and leaned back for greater access.

I then stopped and looked at her and said, "There is a part of me that would like to have sex with you tonight. But it's the part of me that is a seventeen year old boy that had been dreaming of this moment for the past four years."

She tried to persuade me that we could get back together. Things could be the way they were, only better.

"As much as the seventeen year old me in would like that, there is another part of me that wants to have sex with you now out of pure revenge. I would do you and throw you out on the streets before you even had time to dress."

"I guess I have that coming", was all that she could say.

"No. Being bitter over you and what could have been will never help either one of us. So I think you should know that I'm not going to do anything with you that I know I will regret later."

She then tried to convince me that if it was only the one time that we should follow our passions. That's when I told her about my passion.

"I love Liselle. An uncertain future with her is more important to me than our past or my current hatred of you. I'm going to have to ask you to leave."

I watched her get dressed. As she got ready to leave, I could see the tears start to form in her eyes as she said, "We should be planning our wedding right now."

"That future was destroyed a long time ago for me. I've already mourned its loss and moved on."

I kissed her on the cheek and watched her walk away for the last time.

Oct. 29, 2010

I spent all day yesterday expecting Jack to show up and to apologize. About nine o'clock at night, he knocked on the door, handed some stuff to Megan, and then left. He didn't even ask to see me.

He left me a stupid card that said, "Read this. I will be waiting for you at the aquarium on Saturday at eleven o'clock at night. Dress appropriately."

If he loves me, why can't he just say so? All he has to do is come over, tell me that he is sorry, maybe with a box of chocolates and some flowers, and tell me that he loves me. Instead he gives me something to read and a stupid package.

As far as I know, he is still with Brittany. And I refuse to do anything he wants me to do until he comes over and officially apologizes.

In fact, I wouldn't even be reading what he wrote for me tonight as I go to bed, except that Megan says I have to. Apparently Jack has been texting her every hour to see if I have read it yet.

I'll be reading it just for her. It's not going to change anything, though.

The Little Mermaid

By

Jack Webber and Hans Christian Andersen

Far out in the ocean, where the water is as blue as the prettiest eyes, and as clear as crystal, it is very, very deep; so deep, indeed, that no cable could fathom it: many church steeples, piled one upon another, would not reach from the ground beneath to the surface of the water above. There dwell the Sea King and his subjects.

We must not imagine that there is nothing at the bottom of the sea but bare yellow sand. No, indeed; the most singular flowers and plants grow there; the leaves and stems of which are so pliant, that the slightest agitation of the water causes them to stir as if they had life. Fishes, both large and small, glide between the branches, as birds fly among the trees here upon land. In the deepest spot of all, stands the castle of the Sea King.

Its walls are built of coral, and the long, gothic windows are of the clearest amber. The roof is formed of shells, that open and close as the water flows over them. Their appearance is very beautiful, for in each lies a glittering pearl, which would be fit for the crown of a queen.

The Sea King had been a widower for many years, and his aged mother kept house for him. She was a very wise woman, and exceedingly proud of her high birth; on that account she wore twelve oysters on her tail; while others, also of high rank, were only allowed to wear six. She was, however, deserving of very great praise, especially for her care of the little sea-princesses, her grand-daughters.

They were six beautiful children; but the youngest was the prettiest of them all; her skin was as clear and delicate as a rose-leaf, and her eyes as blue as the deepest sea; but, like all the others, she had no feet, and her body ended in a fish's tail.

All day long they played in the great halls of the castle, or among the living flowers that grew out of the walls. The large amber windows were open, and the fish swam in, just as the swallows fly into our houses when we open the windows, excepting that the fishes swam up to the princesses, ate out of their hands, and allowed themselves to be petted.

Outside the castle there was a beautiful garden, in which grew bright red and dark blue flowers, and blossoms like flames of fire; the fruit glittered like gold, and the leaves and stems waved to and fro continually. The earth itself was the finest sand, but blue as the flame of burning sulphur. Over everything lay a peculiar blue radiance, as if it were surrounded by the air from above, through which the blue sky shone, instead of the dark depths of the sea. In calm weather the sun could be seen, looking like a purple flower, with the light streaming from the calyx.

Each of the young princesses had a little plot of ground in the garden, where she might dig and plant as she pleased. One arranged her flower-bed into the form of a whale; another thought it better to make hers like the figure of a little mermaid; but that of the youngest was round like the sun, and contained flowers as red as his rays at sunset.

She was a strange child, quiet and thoughtful; and while her sisters would be delighted with the wonderful things which they obtained from the wrecks of vessels, she cared for nothing but her pretty red flowers, like the sun, excepting a beautiful marble statue.

It was the representation of a handsome boy, carved out of pure white stone, which had fallen to the bottom of the sea from a wreck. She planted by the statue a rose-colored weeping willow. It grew splendidly, and very soon hung its fresh branches over the statue, almost down to the blue sands. The shadow had a violet tint, and waved to and fro like the branches; it seemed as if the crown of the tree and the root were at play, and trying to kiss each other.

Nothing gave her so much pleasure as to hear about the world above the sea. She made her old grandmother tell her all she knew of the ships and of the towns, the people and the animals. To her it seemed most wonderful and beautiful to hear that the flowers of the land should have fragrance, and not those below the sea; that the trees of the forest should be green; and that the fishes among the trees could sing so sweetly, that it was quite a pleasure to hear them. Her grandmother called the little birds fishes, or she would not have understood her; for she had never seen birds.

"When you have reached your fifteenth year," said the grand-mother, "you will have permission to rise up out of the sea, to sit on the rocks in the moonlight, while the great ships are sailing by; and then you will see both forests and towns."

In the following year, one of the sisters would be fifteen: but as each was a year younger than the other, the youngest would have to wait five years before her turn came to rise up from the bottom of the ocean, and see the earth as we do. However, each promised to tell the others what she saw on her first visit, and what she thought the most beautiful; for their grandmother could not tell them enough; there were so many things on which they wanted information. None of them longed so much for her turn to come as the youngest, she who had the longest time to wait, and who was so quiet and thoughtful.

Many nights she stood by the open window, looking up through the dark blue water, and watching the fish as they splashed about with their fins and tails. She could see the moon and stars shining faintly; but through the water they looked larger than they do to our eyes. When something like a black cloud passed between her and them, she knew that it was either a whale swimming over her head, or a ship full of human beings, who never imagined that a pretty little mermaid was standing beneath them, holding out her white hands towards the keel of their ship.

As soon as the eldest was fifteen, she was allowed to rise to the surface of the ocean. When she came back, she had hundreds of things to talk about; but the most beautiful, she said, was to lie in the moonlight, on a sandbank, in the quiet sea, near the coast, and to gaze on a large town nearby, where the lights were twinkling like hundreds of stars; to listen to the sounds of the music, the noise of carriages, and the voices of human beings, and then to hear the merry bells peal out from the church steeples; and because she could not go near to all those wonderful things, she longed for them more than ever. Oh, did not the youngest sister listen eagerly to all these descriptions? and afterwards, when she stood at the open window looking up through the dark blue water, she thought of the great city, with all its bustle and noise, and even fancied she could hear the sound of the church bells, down in the depths of the sea.

In another year the second sister received permission to rise to he surface of the water, and to swim about where she pleased. She rose just as the sun was setting, and this, she said, was the most beautiful sight of all. The whole sky looked like gold, while violet and rose-colored clouds, which she could not describe, floated over her; and, still more rapidly than the clouds, flew a large flock of wild swans towards the setting sun, looking like a long white veil across the sea. She also swam towards the sun; but it sunk into the waves, and the rosy tints faded from the clouds and from the sea.

The third sister's turn followed; she was the boldest of them all, and she swam up a broad river that emptied itself into the sea. On the banks she saw green hills covered with beautiful vines;

palaces and castles peeped out from amid the proud trees of the forest; she heard the birds singing, and the rays of the sun were so powerful that she was obliged often to dive down under the water to cool her burning face.

In a narrow creek she found a whole troop of little human children, quite naked, and sporting about in the water; she wanted to play with them, but they fled in a great fright; and then a little black animal came to the water; it was a dog, but she did not know that, for she had never before seen one. This animal barked at her so terribly that she became frightened, and rushed back to the open sea. But she said she should never forget the beautiful forest, the green hills, and the pretty little children who could swim in the water, although they had not fish's tails.

The fourth sister was more timid; she remained in the midst of the sea, but she said it was quite as beautiful there as nearer the land. She could see for so many miles around her, and the sky above looked like a bell of glass. She had seen the ships, but at such a great distance that they looked like sea-gulls. The dolphins sported in the waves, and the great whales spouted water from their nostrils till it seemed as if a hundred fountains were playing in every direction.

The fifth sister's birthday occurred in the winter; so when her turn came, she saw what the others had not seen the first time they went up. The sea looked quite green, and large icebergs were floating about, each like a pearl, she said, but larger and loftier than the churches built by men. They were of the most singular shapes, and glittered like diamonds. She had seated herself upon one of the largest, and let the wind play with her long hair, and she remarked that all the ships sailed by rapidly, and steered as far away as they could from the iceberg, as if they were afraid of it.

Towards evening, as the sun went down, dark clouds covered the sky, the thunder rolled and the lightning flashed, and the red light glowed on the icebergs as they rocked and tossed on the heaving sea. On all the ships the sails were reefed with fear and trembling, while she sat calmly on the floating iceberg, watching the blue lightning, as it darted its forked flashes into the sea.

When first the sisters had permission to rise to the surface, they were each delighted with the new and beautiful sights they saw; but now, as grown-up girls, they could go when they pleased, and they had become indifferent about it. They wished themselves back again in the water, and after a month had passed they said it was much more beautiful down below, and pleasanter to be at home.

Yet often, in the evening hours, the five sisters would twine their arms round each other, and rise to the surface, in a row. They had more beautiful voices than any human being could have; and before the approach of a storm, and when they expected a ship would be lost, they swam before the vessel, and sang sweetly of the delights to be found in the depths of the sea, and begging the sailors not to fear if they sank to the bottom. But the sailors could not understand the song, they took it for the howling of the storm. And these things were never to be beautiful for them; for if the ship sank, the men were drowned, and their dead bodies alone reached the palace of the Sea King.

When the sisters rose, arm-in-arm, through the water in this way, their youngest sister would stand quite alone, looking after them, ready to cry, only that the mermaids have no tears, and therefore they suffer more. "Oh, were I but fifteen years old," said she: "I know that I shall love the world up there, and all the people who live in it."

At last she reached her fifteenth year. "Well, now, you are grown up," said the old dowager, her grandmother; "so you must let me adorn you like your other sisters;" and she placed a wreath of white lilies in her hair, and every flower leaf was half a pearl. Then the old lady ordered eight great oysters to attach themselves to the tail of the princess to show her high rank.

"But they hurt me so," said the little mermaid.

"Pride must suffer pain," replied the old lady. Oh, how gladly she would have shaken off all this grandeur, and laid aside the heavy wreath! The red flowers in her own garden would have suited her much better, but she could not help herself: so she said, "Farewell," and rose as lightly as a bubble to the surface of the water. The sun had just set as she raised her head above the waves; but the clouds were tinted with crimson and gold, and through the glimmering twilight beamed the evening star in all its beauty. The sea was calm, and the air mild and fresh. A large ship, with three masts, lay becalmed on the water, with only one sail set; for not a breeze stiffed, and the sailors sat idle on deck or amongst the rigging. There was music and song on board; and, as darkness came on, a hundred colored lanterns were lighted, as if the flags of all nations waved in the air.

The little mermaid swam close to the cabin windows; and now and then, as the waves lifted her up, she could look in through clear glass window-panes, and see a number of well-dressed people within. Among them was a young prince, the most beautiful of all, with large black eyes; he was sixteen years of age, and his birthday was being kept with much rejoicing. The sailors were dancing on deck, but when the prince came out of the cabin, more than a hundred rockets rose in the air, making it as bright as day.

The little mermaid was so startled that she dived under water; and when she again stretched out her head, it appeared as if all the stars of heaven were falling around her, she had never seen such fireworks before. Great suns spurted fire about, splendid fireflies flew into the blue air, and everything was reflected in the clear, calm sea beneath. The ship itself was so brightly illuminated that all the people, and even the smallest rope, could be distinctly and plainly seen. And how handsome the young prince looked, as he pressed the hands of all present and smiled at them, while the music resounded through the clear night air.

It was very late; yet the little mermaid could not take her eyes from the ship, or from the beautiful prince. The colored lanterns had been extinguished, no more rockets rose in the air, and the cannon had ceased firing; but the sea became restless, and a moaning, grumbling sound could be heard beneath the waves: still the little mermaid remained by the cabin window, rocking up and down on the water, which enabled her to look in.

After a while, the sails were quickly unfurled, and the noble ship continued her passage; but soon the waves rose higher, heavy clouds darkened the sky, and lightning appeared in the distance. A dreadful storm was approaching; once more the sails were reefed, and the great ship pursued her flying course over the raging sea. The waves rose mountains high, as if they would have overtopped the mast; but the ship dived like a swan between them, and then rose again on their lofty, foaming crests. To the little mermaid this appeared pleasant sport; not so to the sailors.

At length the ship groaned and creaked; the thick planks gave way under the lashing of the sea as it broke over the deck; the mainmast snapped asunder like a reed; the ship lay over on her side; and the water rushed in. The little mermaid now perceived that the crew was in danger; even she herself was obliged to be careful to avoid the beams and planks of the wreck which lay scattered on the water. At one moment it was so pitch dark that she could not see a single object, but a flash of lightning revealed the whole scene; she could see everyone who had been on board excepting the prince; when the ship parted, she had seen him sink into the deep waves, and she was glad, for she thought he would now be with her; and then she remembered that human beings could not live in the water, so that when he got down to her father's palace he would be quite dead.

But he must not die. So she swam about among the beams and planks which strewed the surface of the sea, forgetting that they could crush her to pieces. Then she dived deeply under the dark waters, rising and falling with the waves, till at length she managed to reach the young prince, who was fast losing the power of swimming in that stormy sea. His limbs were failing him, his beautiful eyes were closed, and he would have died had not the little mermaid come to his assistance. She held his head above the water, and let the waves drift them where they would.

In the morning the storm had ceased; but of the ship not a single fragment could be seen. The sun rose up red and glowing from the water, and its beams brought back the hue of health to the prince's cheeks; but his eyes remained closed. The mermaid kissed his high, smooth forehead, and stroked back his wet hair; he seemed to her like the marble statue in her little garden, and she kissed him again, and wished that he might live.

Presently they came in sight of land; she saw lofty blue mountains, on which the white snow rested as if a flock of swans were lying upon them. Near the coast were beautiful green forests, and close by stood a large building, whether a church or a convent she could not tell. Orange and citron trees grew in the garden, and before the door stood lofty palms.

The sea here formed a little bay, in which the water was quite still, but very deep; so she swam with the handsome prince to the beach, which was covered with fine, white sand, and there she laid him in the warm sunshine, taking care to raise his head higher than his body.

Then bells sounded in the large white building, and a number of young girls came into the garden. The little mermaid swam out farther from the shore and placed herself between some high rocks that rose out of the water; then she covered her head and neck with the foam of the sea so that her little face might not be seen, and watched to see what would become of the poor prince.

She did not wait long before she saw a young girl approach the spot where he lay. She seemed frightened at first, but only for a moment; then she fetched a number of people, and the mermaid saw that the prince came to life again, and smiled upon those who stood round him. But to her he sent no smile; he knew not that she had saved him. This made her very unhappy, and when he was led away into the great building, she dived down sorrowfully into the water, and returned to her father's castle.

She had always been silent and thoughtful, and now she was more so than ever. Her sisters asked her what she had seen during her first visit to the surface of the water; but she would tell them nothing. Many an evening and morning she would rise to the place where she had left the prince. She saw the fruits in the garden ripen till they were gathered, the snow on the tops of the mountains melt away; but she never saw the prince, and therefore she returned home, always more sorrowful than before.

It was her only comfort to sit in her own little garden, and fling her arm round the beautiful marble statue which was like the prince; but she gave up tending her flowers, and they grew in wild confusion over the paths, twining their long leaves and stems round the branches of the trees, so that the whole place became dark and gloomy.

At length she could bear it no longer, and told one of her sisters all about it. Then the others heard the secret, and very soon it became known to two mermaids whose intimate friend happened to know who the prince was. She had also seen the festival on board ship, and she told them where the prince came from, and where his palace stood.

"Come, little sister," said the other princesses; then they entwined their arms and rose up in a long row to the surface of the water, close by the spot where they knew the prince's palace stood.

It was built of bright yellow shining stone, with long flights of marble steps, one of which reached quite down to the sea. Splendid gilded cupolas rose over the roof, and between the pillars that surrounded the whole building stood life-like statues of marble.

Through the clear crystal of the lofty windows could be seen noble rooms, with costly silk curtains and hangings of tapestry; while the walls were covered with beautiful paintings which were a pleasure to look at. In the centre of the largest saloon a fountain threw its sparkling jets high up into the glass cupola of the ceiling, through which the sun shone down upon the water and upon the beautiful plants growing round the basin of the fountain.

Now that she knew where he lived, she spent many an evening and many a night on the water near the palace. She would swim much nearer the shore than any of the others ventured to do; indeed once she went quite up the narrow channel under the marble balcony, which threw a broad shadow on the water.

Here she would sit and watch the young prince, who thought himself quite alone in the bright moonlight. She saw him many times of an evening sailing in a pleasant boat, with music playing and flags waving. She peeped out from among the green rushes, and if the wind caught her long silvery-white veil, those who saw it believed it to be a swan, spreading out its wings. On many a night, too, when the fishermen, with their torches, were out at sea, she heard them relate so many good things about the doings of the young prince, that she was glad she had saved his life when he had been tossed about half-dead on the waves.

And she remembered that his head had rested on her bosom, and how heartily she had kissed him; but he knew nothing of all this, and could not even dream of her. She grew more and more fond of human beings, and wished more and more to be able to wander about with those whose world seemed to be so much larger than her own.

They could fly over the sea in ships, and mount the high hills which were far above the clouds; and the lands they possessed, their woods and their fields, stretched far away beyond the reach of her sight.

There was so much that she wished to know, and her sisters were unable to answer all her questions. Then she applied to her old grandmother, who knew all about the upper world, which she very rightly called the lands above the sea.

"If human beings are not drowned," asked the little mermaid, "can they live forever? Do they never die as we do here in the sea?"

"Yes," replied the old lady, "they must also die, and their term of life is even shorter than ours. We sometimes live to three hundred years, but when we cease to exist here we only become the foam on the surface of the water, and we have not even a grave down here of those we love. We have not immortal souls, we shall never live again; but, like the green sea-weed, when once it has been cut off, we can never flourish more. Human beings, on the contrary, have a soul which lives forever, lives after the body has been turned to dust. It rises up through the clear, pure air beyond the glittering stars. As we rise out of the water, and behold all the land of the earth, so do they rise to unknown and glorious regions which we shall never see."

"Why have not we an immortal soul?" asked the little mermaid mournfully; "I would give gladly all the hundreds of years that I have to live, to be a human being only for one day, and to have the hope of knowing the happiness of that glorious world above the stars."

"You must not think of that," said the old woman; "we feel ourselves to be much happier and much better off than human beings."

"So I shall die," said the little mermaid, "and as the foam of the sea I shall be driven about never again to hear the music of the waves, or to see the pretty flowers nor the red sun. Is there anything I can do to win an immortal soul?"

"No," said the old woman, "unless a man were to love you so much that you were more to him than his father or mother; and if all his thoughts and all his love were fixed upon you, and the priest placed his right hand in yours, and he promised to be true to you here and hereafter, then his soul would glide into your body and you would obtain a share in the future happiness of mankind. He would give a soul to you and retain his own as well; but this can never happen. Your fish's tail, which amongst us is considered so beautiful, is thought on earth to be quite ugly; they do not know any better, and they think it necessary to have two stout props, which they call legs, in order to be beautiful."

Then the little mermaid sighed, and looked sorrowfully at her fish's tail. "Let us be happy," said the old lady, "and dart and spring about during the three hundred years that we have to live, which is really quite long enough; after that we can rest ourselves all the better. This evening we are going to have a court ball."

It is one of those splendid sights which we can never see on earth. The walls and the ceiling of the large ball-room were of thick, but transparent crystal. Many hundreds of colossal shells, some of a deep red, others of a grass green, stood on each side in rows, with blue fire in them, which lighted up the whole saloon, and shone through the walls, so that the sea was also illuminated. Innumerable fishes, great and small, swam past the crystal walls; on some of them the scales glowed with a purple brilliancy, and on others they shone like silver and gold. Through the halls flowed a broad stream, and in it danced the mermen and the mermaids to the music of their own sweet singing.

No one on earth has such a lovely voice as theirs. The little mermaid sang more sweetly than them all. The whole court applauded her with hands and tails; and for a moment her heart felt quite gay, for she knew she had the loveliest voice of any on earth or in the sea. But she soon thought again of the world above her, for she could not forget the charming prince, nor her sorrow that she had not an immortal soul like his; therefore she crept away silently out of her father's palace, and while everything within was gladness and song, she sat in her own little garden sorrowful and alone.

Then she heard the bugle sounding through the water, and thought--"He is certainly sailing above, he on whom my wishes depend, and in whose hands I should like to place the happiness of my life. I will venture all for him, and to win an immortal soul, while my sisters are dancing in my father's palace, I will go to the sea witch, of whom I have always been so much afraid, but she can give me counsel and help."

And then the little mermaid went out from her garden, and took the road to the foaming whirlpools, behind which the sorceress lived. She had never been that way before: neither flowers nor grass grew there; nothing but bare, gray, sandy ground stretched out to the whirlpool, where the water, like foaming mill-wheels, whirled round everything that it seized, and cast it into the fathomless deep.

Through the midst of these crushing whirlpools the little mermaid was obliged to pass, to reach the dominions of the sea witch; and also for a long distance the only road lay right across a quantity of warm, bubbling mire, called by the witch her turfmoor. Beyond this stood her house, in the centre of a strange forest, in which all the trees and flowers were polypi, half animals and half plants; they looked like serpents with a hundred heads growing out of the ground.

The branches were long slimy arms, with fingers like flexible worms, moving limb after limb from the root to the top. All that could be reached in the sea they seized upon, and held fast, so that it never escaped from their clutches.

The little mermaid was so alarmed at what she saw, that she stood still, and her heart beat with fear, and she was very nearly turning back; but she thought of the prince, and of the human soul for which she longed, and her courage returned. She fastened her long flowing hair round her head, so that the polypi might not seize hold of it.

She laid her hands together across her bosom, and then she darted forward as a fish shoots through the water, between the supple arms and fingers of the ugly polypi, which were stretched out on each side of her. She saw that each held in its grasp something it had seized with its numerous little arms, as if they were iron bands. The white skeletons of human beings who had perished at sea, and had sunk down into the deep waters, skeletons of land animals, oars, rudders, and chests of ships were lying tightly grasped by their clinging arms; even a little mermaid, whom they had caught and strangled; and this seemed the most shocking of all to the little princess.

She now came to a space of marshy ground in the wood, where large, fat water-snakes were rolling in the mire, and showing their ugly, drab-colored bodies. In the midst of this spot stood a house, built with the bones of shipwrecked human beings. There sat the sea witch, allowing a toad to eat from her mouth, just as people sometimes feed a canary with a piece of sugar. She called the ugly water-snakes her little chickens, and allowed them to crawl all over her bosom.

"I know what you want," said the sea witch; "it is very stupid of you, but you shall have your way, and it will bring you to sorrow, my pretty princess. You want to get rid of your fish's tail, and to have two supports instead of it, like human beings on earth, so that the young prince may fall in love with you, and that you may have an immortal soul." And then the witch laughed so loud and disgustingly, that the toad and the snakes fell to the ground, and lay there wriggling about.

"You are but just in time," said the witch; "for after sunrise to-morrow I should not be able to help you till the end of another year. I will prepare a draught for you, with which you must swim to land tomorrow before sunrise, and sit down on the shore and drink it. Your tail will then disappear, and shrink up into what mankind calls legs, and you will feel great pain, as if a sword were passing through you. But all who see you will say that you are the prettiest little human being they ever saw. You will still have the same floating gracefulness of movement, and no dancer will ever tread so lightly; but at every step you take it will feel as if you were treading upon sharp knives, and that the blood must flow. If you will bear all this, I will help you."

"Yes, I will," said the little princess in a trembling voice, as she thought of the prince and the immortal soul.

"But think again," said the witch; "for when once your shape has become like a human being, you can no more be a mermaid. You will never return through the water to your sisters, or to your father's palace again; and if you do not win the love of the prince, so that he is willing to forget his father and mother for your sake, and to love you with his whole soul, and allow the priest to join your hands that you may be man and wife, then you will never have an immortal soul. The first morning after he marries another your heart will break, and you will become foam on the crest of the waves."

"I will do it," said the little mermaid, and she became pale as death.

"But I must be paid also," said the witch, "and it is not a trifle that I ask. You have the sweetest voice of any who dwell here in the depths of the sea, and you believe that you will be able to charm the prince with it also, but this voice you must give to me; the best thing you possess will I have for the price of my draught. My own blood must be mixed with it, that it may be as sharp as a two-edged sword."

"But if you take away my voice," said the little mermaid, "what is left for me?"

"Your beautiful form, your graceful walk, and your expressive eyes; surely with these you can enchain a man's heart. Well, have you lost your courage? Sing for me so as may take my payment; then you shall have the powerful draught."

"It shall be," said the little mermaid.

Then the witch placed her cauldron on the fire, to prepare the magic draught.

"Cleanliness is a good thing," said she, scouring the vessel with snakes, which she had tied together in a large knot; then she pricked herself in the breast, and let the black blood drop into it.

The steam that rose formed itself into such horrible shapes that no one could look at them without fear. Every moment the witch threw something else into the vessel, and when it began to boil, the sound was like the weeping of a crocodile. When at last the magic draught as ready, it looked like the clearest water.

"There it is for you," said the witch. "If the polypi should seize hold of you as you return through the wood," said the witch, "throw over them a few drops of the potion, and their fingers will be torn into a thousand pieces." But the little mermaid had no occasion to do this, for the polypi sprang back in terror when they caught sight of the glittering draught, which shone in her hand like a twinkling star.

So she passed quickly through the wood and the marsh, and between the rushing whirlpools. She saw that in her father's palace the torches in the ballroom were extinguished, and all within asleep; but she did not venture to go in to them, for now she was mute and going to leave them forever, she felt as if her heart would break.

She stole into the garden, took a flower from the flower-beds of each of her sisters, kissed her hand a thousand times towards the palace, and then rose up through the dark blue waters. The sun had not risen when she came in sight of the prince's palace, and approached the beautiful marble steps, but the moon shone clear and bright.

Then the little mermaid drank the magic draught, and it seemed as if a two-edged sword went through her delicate body: she fell into a swoon, and lay like one dead. When the sun arose and shone over the sea, she recovered, and felt a sharp pain; but just before her stood the handsome young prince. He fixed his coal-black eyes upon her so earnestly that she cast down her own, and then became aware that her fish's tail was gone, and that she had as pretty a pair of white legs and tiny feet as any little maiden could have; but she had no clothes, so she wrapped herself in her long, thick hair.

The prince asked her who she was, and where she came from, and she looked at him mildly and sorrowfully with her deep blue eyes; but she could not speak. Every step she took was as the witch had said it would be, she felt as if treading upon the points of needles or sharp knives; but she bore it willingly, and stepped as lightly by the prince's side as a soap-bubble, so that he and all who saw her wondered at her graceful-swaying movements. She was very soon arrayed in costly robes of silk and muslin, and was the most beautiful creature in the palace; but she could neither speak nor sing.

Beautiful female slaves, dressed in silk and gold, stepped forward and sang before the prince and his royal parents: one sang better than all the others, and the prince clapped his hands and smiled at her.

This was great sorrow to the little mermaid; she knew how much more sweetly she herself could sing once, and she thought, "Oh if he could only know that! I have given away my voice forever, to be with him."

The slaves next performed some pretty fairy-like dances, to the sound of beautiful music.

Then the little mermaid raised her lovely white arms, stood on the tips of her toes, and glided over the floor, and danced as no one yet had been able to dance. At each moment her beauty became more revealed, and her expressive eyes appealed more directly to the heart than the songs of the slaves.

Everyone was enchanted, especially the prince, who called her his little foundling; and she danced again quite readily, to please him, though each time her foot touched the floor it seemed as if she trod on sharp knives.

The prince said she should remain with him always, and she received permission to sleep at his door, on a velvet cushion. He had a page's dress made for her, that she might accompany him on horseback. They rode together through the sweet-scented woods, where the green boughs touched their shoulders, and the little birds sang among the fresh leaves. She climbed with the prince to the tops of high mountains; and although her tender feet bled so that even her steps were marked, she only laughed, and followed him till they could see the clouds beneath them looking like a flock of birds travelling to distant lands.

While at the prince's palace, and when all the household were asleep, she would go and sit on the broad marble steps; for it eased her burning feet to bathe them in the cold sea-water; and then she thought of all those below in the deep.

Once during the night her sisters came up arm-in-arm, singing sorrowfully, as they floated on the water. She beckoned to them, and then they recognized her, and told her how she had grieved them. After that, they came to the same place every night; and once she saw in the distance her old grandmother, who had not been to the surface of the sea for many years, and the old Sea King, her father, with his crown on his head. They stretched out their hands towards her, but they did not venture so near the land as her sisters did.

As the days passed, she loved the prince more fondly, and he loved her as he would love a little child, but it never came into his head to make her his wife; yet, unless he married her, she could not receive an immortal soul; and, on the morning after his marriage with another, she would dissolve into the foam of the sea.

"Do you not love me the best of them all?" the eyes of the little mermaid seemed to say, when he took her in his arms, and kissed her fair forehead.

"Yes, you are dear to me," said the prince; "for you have the best heart, and you are the most devoted to me; you are like a young maiden whom

I once saw, but whom I shall never meet again. I was in a ship that was wrecked, and the waves cast me ashore near a holy temple, where several young maidens performed the service. The youngest of them found me on the shore, and saved my life. I saw her but twice, and she is the only one in the world whom I could love; but you are like her, and you have almost driven her image out of my mind. She belongs to the holy temple, and my good fortune has sent you to me instead of her; and we will never part."

"Ah, he knows not that it was I who saved his life," thought the little mermaid. "I carried him over the sea to the wood where the temple stands: I sat beneath the foam, and watched till the human beings came to help him. I saw the pretty maiden that he loves better than he loves me;" and the mermaid sighed deeply, but she could not shed tears. "He says the maiden belongs to the holy temple, therefore she will never return to the world. They will meet no more: while I am by his side, and see him every day. I will take care of him, and love him, and give up my life for his sake."

Very soon it was said that the prince must marry, and that the beautiful daughter of a neighboring king would be his wife, for a fine ship was being fitted out. Although the prince gave out that he merely intended to pay a visit to the king, it was generally supposed that he really went to see his daughter. A great company was to go with him. The little mermaid smiled, and shook her head. She knew the prince's thoughts better than any of the others.

"I must travel," he had said to her; "I must see this beautiful princess; my parents desire it; but they will not oblige me to bring her home as my bride. I cannot love her; she is not like the beautiful maiden in the temple, whom you resemble. If I were forced to choose a bride, I would rather choose you, my mute foundling, with those expressive eyes." And then he kissed her rosy mouth, played with her long waving hair, and laid his head on her heart, while she dreamed of human happiness and an immortal soul. "You are not afraid of the sea, my mute child," said he, as they stood on the deck of the noble ship which was to carry them to the country of the neighboring king.

And then he told her of storm and of calm, of strange fishes in the deep beneath them, and of what the divers had seen there; and she smiled at his descriptions, for she knew better than anyone what wonders were at the bottom of the sea.

In the moonlight, when all on board were asleep, excepting the man at the helm, who was steering, she sat on the deck, gazing down through the clear water. She thought she could distinguish her father's castle, and upon it her aged grandmother, with the silver crown on her head, looking through the rushing tide at the keel of the vessel. Then her sisters came up on the waves, and gazed at her mournfully, wringing their white hands. She beckoned to them, and smiled, and wanted to tell them how happy and well off she was; but the cabin-boy approached, and when her sisters dived down he thought it was only the foam of the sea which he saw.

The next morning the ship sailed into the harbor of a beautiful town belonging to the king whom the prince was going to visit. The church bells were ringing, and from the high towers sounded a flourish of trumpets; and soldiers, with flying colors and glittering bayonets, lined the rocks through which they passed. Every day was a festival; balls and entertainments followed one another.

But the princess had not yet appeared. People said that she was being brought up and educated in a religious house, where she was learning every royal virtue. At last she came. Then the little mermaid, who was very anxious to see whether she was really beautiful, was obliged to acknowledge that she had never seen a more perfect vision of beauty. Her skin was delicately fair, and beneath her long dark eye-lashes her laughing blue eyes shone with truth and purity.

"It was you," said the prince, "who saved my life when I lay dead on the beach," and he folded his blushing bride in his arms. "Oh, I am too happy," said he to the little mermaid; "my fondest hopes are all fulfilled. You will rejoice at my happiness; for your devotion to me is great and sincere."

The little mermaid kissed his hand, and felt as if her heart were already broken. His wedding morning would bring death to her, and she would change into the foam of the sea. All the church bells rung and the heralds rode about the town proclaiming the betrothal.

Perfumed oil was burning in costly silver lamps on every altar. The priests waved the censers, while the bride and bridegroom joined their hands and received the blessing of the bishop. The little mermaid, dressed in silk and gold, held up the bride's train; but her ears heard nothing of the festive music, and her eyes saw not the holy ceremony; she thought of the night of death which was coming to her, and of all she had lost in the world. On the same evening the bride and bridegroom went on board ship; cannons were roaring, flags waving, and in the centre of the ship a costly tent of purple and gold had been erected. It contained elegant couches, for the reception of the bridal pair during the night. The ship, with swelling sails and a favorable wind, glided away smoothly and lightly over the calm sea.

When it grew dark a number of colored lamps were lit, and the sailors danced merrily on the deck. The little mermaid could not help thinking of her first rising out of the sea, when she had seen similar festivities and joys; and she joined in the dance, poised herself in the air as a swallow when he pursues his prey, and all present cheered her with wonder. She had never danced so elegantly before. Her tender feet felt as if cut with sharp knives, but she cared not for it; a sharper pang had pierced through her heart. She knew this was the last evening she should ever see the prince, for whom she had forsaken her kindred and her home; she had given up her beautiful voice, and suffered unheard-of pain daily for him, while he knew nothing of it. This was the last evening that she would breathe the same air with him, or gaze on the starry sky and the deep sea; an eternal night, without a thought or a dream, awaited her: she had no soul and now she could never win one. All was joy and gayety on board ship till long after midnight; she laughed and danced with the rest, while the thoughts of death were in her heart.

The prince kissed his beautiful bride, while she played with his raven hair, till they went arm-in-arm to rest in the splendid tent. Then all became still on board the ship; the helmsman, alone awake, stood at the helm. The little mermaid leaned her white arms on the edge of the vessel, and looked towards the east for the first blush of morning, for that first ray of dawn that would bring her death. She saw her sisters rising out of the flood: they were as pale as herself; but their long beautiful hair waved no more in the wind, and had been cut off.

"We have given our hair to the witch," said they, "to obtain help for you, that you may not die to-night. She has given us a knife: here it is, see it is very sharp. Before the sun rises you must plunge it into the heart of the prince; when the warm blood falls upon your feet they will grow together again, and form into a fish's tail, and you will be once more a mermaid, and return to us to live out your three hundred years before you die and change into the salt sea foam. Haste, then; he or you must die before sunrise. Our old grandmother moans so for you, that her white hair is falling off from sorrow, as ours fell under the witch's scissors. Kill the prince and come back; hasten: do you not see the first red streaks in the sky? In a few minutes the sun will rise, and you must die." And then they sighed deeply and mournfully, and sank down beneath the waves.

The little mermaid drew back the crimson curtain of the tent, and beheld the fair bride with her head resting on the prince's breast. She bent down and kissed his fair brow, then looked at the sky on which the rosy dawn grew brighter and brighter; then she glanced at the sharp knife, and again fixed her eyes on the prince, who whispered the name of his bride in his dreams. She was in his thoughts, and the knife trembled in the hand of the little mermaid: then she flung it far away from her into the waves; the water turned red where it fell, and the drops that spurted up looked like blood.

She cast one more lingering, half-fainting glance at the prince, and then threw herself from the ship into the sea, and thought her body was dissolving into foam. The sun rose above the waves, and his warm rays fell on the cold foam of the little mermaid, who did not feel as if she were dying. She saw the bright sun, and all around her floated hundreds of transparent beautiful beings; she could see through them the white sails of the ship, and the red clouds in the sky; their speech was melodious, but too ethereal to be heard by mortal ears, as they were also unseen by mortal eyes.

The little mermaid perceived that she had a body like theirs, and that she continued to rise higher and higher out of the foam. "Where am I?" asked she, and her voice sounded ethereal, as the voice of those who were with her; no earthly music could imitate it.

"Among the daughters of the air," answered one of them. "A mermaid has not an immortal soul, nor can she obtain one unless she wins the love of a human being. On the power of another hangs her eternal destiny. But the daughters of the air, although they do not possess an immortal soul, can, by their good deeds, procure one for themselves. We fly to warm countries, and cool the sultry air that destroys mankind with the pestilence. We carry the perfume of the flowers to spread health and restoration. After we have striven for three hundred years to all the good in our power, we receive an immortal soul and take part in the happiness of mankind. You, poor little mermaid, have tried with your whole heart to do as we are doing; you have suffered and endured and raised yourself to the spirit-world by your good deeds; and now, by striving for three hundred years in the same way, you may obtain an immortal soul."

The little mermaid lifted her glorified eyes towards the sun, and felt them, for the first time, filling with tears. On the ship, in which she had left the prince, there were life and noise; she saw him and his beautiful bride searching for her; sorrowfully they gazed at the pearly foam, as if they knew she had thrown herself into the waves. Unseen she kissed the forehead of his bride, and fanned the prince, and then mounted with the other children of the air to a rosy cloud that floated through the aether.

"After three hundred years, thus shall we float into the kingdom of heaven," said she. "And we may even get there sooner," whispered one of her companions. "Unseen we can enter the houses of men, where there are children, and for every day on which we find a good child, who is the joy of his parents and deserves their love, our time of probation is shortened. The child does not know, when we fly through the room, that we smile with joy at his good conduct, for we can count one year less of our three hundred years. But when we see a naughty or a wicked child, we shed tears of sorrow, and for every tear a day is added to our time of trial!"

Dear Liselle,

This is the original version of the story that you love so much. I don't have dark hair or blue eyes. Although Brittany may have presented herself as somebody pure when I was dating her, I knew about her past when I was with you.

If you want any part of this story to be true for us, you will have to accept that when it came time for me to decide which girl that I wanted to marry that I chose the little mermaid.

I was busy preparing this story for you the morning that you fought Brittany and walked out on me. Despite what she might have told you, I told her that I felt nothing for her anymore. I don't know why she told you that, except that she was trying to get me back.

If you want the proper ending to this story (the ending you've been wanting all of your life), meet me at the aquarium Saturday night at 11:00 pm.

I will be waiting for you at the spot where you found your voice and were able to tell me that you loved me.

Jack

Oct. 30, 2010

At eleven o'clock at night, I entered the aquarium wearing the clam shell bra and fishtail bottom that Jack had left for me. He was standing in the very spot where I had shouted my love him. He was dressed like a prince, but even the royal clothes could not hide his fear that I wouldn't show up. His fear faded the moment that he saw me. Seeing his smile, the relief on his face, and the joy that my presence had brought him would have been enough to forgive him for everything that he didn't do the past two days.

As I ran towards him, I started to speak, but he stopped me by putting his finger gently to my lips and saying, "You can't speak. You've given up your voice for a chance to be with me."

I couldn't help but to blush a little. Some people were looking at us, but I didn't care. I was about to get my happy ending.

"I'm sorry if I kept looking for that girl that I thought had saved me, when it was really you. When I started to realize that I had feelings for you, I should have told you about it. Instead, I made you wonder what my true feelings were when we broke up. This let Brittany mess with your head and make you doubt me. I can never really make that up to you." He then got down on one knee, brought out the ring, and said, "Will you be my girlfriend? Not because we are pretending to be a couple, but because I love you."

With everything that was happening, I was speechless. I think my not speaking started to bother him. He said, "You can talk now."

I kissed him and said, "Yes. I will be your girlfriend for real this time."

He then put the ring on my finger and said, "I want this to be a reminder of how we met and how it took me a little too long to realize that you were the girl that I had been searching for."

And then, with all of the things that I wanted to do to him, I thought that it was best to go back to my place. And although we were starting to get pretty hot and heavy, I stopped him and said, "I've been with more guys than I would care to admit. Since this is going to be your first time, I want it to be special."

"You're dressed like a mermaid, and I'm dressed like a prince. I would call that pretty special."

"I want you to have the experience that I should have had. I know that it probably isn't important to you, but it will be my first time with a guy that actually cares for me. I want it to be special."

And he held me close, kissed me tenderly, as we talked about all of the stupid things that we can always seem to talk about.

A Lover's Question
By
Jack Webber

She steps into the bedroom like a ghost trapped forever within its own personal hell that can never be free of that certain time and place.

Although there is sorrow on her face, her beauty shines through. Her stunning hazel eyes, long brown hair, and soft pink lips invite you towards her.

And as she stands there looking at you, the bedroom door slowly closes. You aren't really sure how it happened. You are too busy watching her disrobe and revealing her magnificent flesh that reminds you both that you are human and that the moment you are lost in is now.

Do you think I'm beautiful?

You want to speak, but words fail you. So you walk over to her. You start to look her in the eyes as you play with her hair. As she longs for an answer, you can no longer take her gaze, which searches your soul. You find yourself looking at her lips and wanting to kiss her, but you know you should answer her question first.

As the smell of her perfume fills your senses and you feel her breathing increase with the beating of her heart as she waits for your answer, you are so entranced by her and everything that she means to you that you try to tell her what you've always thought and have left unspoken.

You pray that her feelings for you make your confused thoughts perfect to her ears.

> *I've always thought you were beautiful. I just… I'm sorry if I made you think that you had to do your hair, makeup, and undress to get me to say the very things I have been thinking each morning as you wake up next to me.*

Between admitting the thoughts you have been trying to discount for so long and her total command of the situation as she moves in still closer to you, you become more uncomfortable as the demons you have been trying to control for so long start to come to the surface.

> *Do you love me?*

It is in that moment that you realize that you were never really afraid of loving her. You were terrified that you weren't worthy of her and her affections.

It is then that you realize that she isn't the ghost that is trapped in its own memory. You are. Hurt by love, you have refused to come towards her light and leave the life you once knew behind and move into the Great Unknown with her.

Do you give up your past life that no longer has use of you, or do you hold onto it with an iron grip knowing that it has been your security blanket for so long?

As the forces of good and evil wage a heavenly battle for your soul, you look at the woman in front of you. You see how she waits for your answer. She wants nothing more than to hear you say the words she has already said to you. As she stands naked before you, you realize she has only hope at that moment, as she pleads silently:

> *Let me love you. I can love you. I will always love you.*

And a voice from a distant past whispers in your ear:

> *Hold on to me. I feel you slipping away from me. If you let go of me, I can never come back to you.*

As you start to waiver, that distant voice makes another attempt:

She can never love you like I loved you.

As the small glimmer of hope starts to fade from the woman in front of you, you find your answer.

As unworthy, broken, and scared as I am right now, the only thing that I can be certain of is the fact that I love you.

As her body presses up against yours, you become aware of the warmth coming from your heart and hers. As it envelops you, you let go of the fear that had been holding you back. As she kisses you, you step fully into the light and into eternity.

About This Novel

As a writer, I oftentimes get an idea for my next work while I am working on one piece, or shortly after having finished one piece. I find that there are ideas, themes, and other small things that I didn't fully explore with the first piece. I pick these up in the new work and look at them from a different perspective or develop them in another way. I have always found that there are two or three different ways a story could go. Sometimes the path that I do not take in one story leads me to an idea for another story.

This is the case with *Broken Hearts Damaged Goods*. In many ways, it is the companion piece to *Fairy Tale Romance*. The two are similar in that both have a man and a woman that do not really know each other living together.

With *Fairy Tale Romance*, I was interested in the idea of telling four different fairy tales and intercutting them into a single narrative. This could only exist as a film because of the need to show that the different characters in the fairy tales were really the same person.

Broken Hearts Damaged Goods originally started out as a film as well. I had intended it to be a poetic film with Jack and Liselle developing their relationship in bed. It was going to be told primarily through their conversations in bed.

The script for this was started sometime around 2005 or 2006. It was only completed up to the point where Jack and Liselle are in the shower the night of the beer pong competition against Steve and Brittany. It was then abandoned. It was virtually impossible to write a poetic film with the majority of the dialogue happening in the bedroom.

With some time and distance between *Fairy Tale Romance*, I decided to pick up *Broken Hearts Damaged Goods* again, but this time as a novel. Although it might share some similarities with *Fairy Tale Romance*, I was more interested in telling the story of a couple as they try to heal from their previous relationships.

My interest was in the idea of the cocoon, with *Cocoon* being the original title of the work. I wanted to see what caused the couple to go into this protective state, how they changed once they were inside of it, and how they would have to cope with the changes once they emerged from it.

About the Author

Jack Gunthridge is single. He is just throwing that out there since the majority of authors talk about how they are happily married, have a certain number kids, and a few pets. Jack doesn't have a girlfriend, and he once had a tank of sea-monkeys die on him. This does make writing these "About the Author" sections harder to write. He doesn't consider himself a failure, though. He just hasn't met the right girl. So if you think you would like to date him, you might end up in his next "About the Author" section.

Although he is becoming more well known for his books, Jack actually defines himself as a writer/director and feels more comfortable with his film and TV work than as an author. He spends the majority of his free time watching movies and TV. In fact, Hollywood has had a greater influence on his career than books.

Never one to disappoint his fans, he is spending more time these days writing novels. His next novel is going to be a paranormal romance. Not one to usually follow trends, Jack Gunthridge decided that the paranormal romance genre needed a reworking. Plus his idea for the story comes from a short story that he wrote before there was a trend.

If you would like to know more about Jack Gunthridge, you can find him on FaceBook, or check out his website: http://www.jackgunthridge.com. You can also write to him at jackgunthridge@hotmail.com.

He enjoys hearing from his fans and responds to all messages personally. If you want a letter with his actual signature, you can write to him at:

P.O. Box 1439
Bowling Green, OH 43402

<u>Other Works</u>

Books
Life

Films
(Available on DVD)
Thursday
Fairy Tale Romance

And look for more episodes of
The Gunthridge Show
coming soon with previous seasons already available on DVD.

www.ingramcontent.com/pod-product-compliance
Lightning Source LLC
Chambersburg PA
CBHW030819310726
48980CB00006B/555/J

* 9 7 8 0 6 1 5 5 0 4 6 2 9 *